The Piemakers

Arthy, Jem, and Gravella Roller are the finest pie-makers in Danby Dale, famed for their perfect pastry and fantastic fillings. So when they're asked to make a special pie for the king, which will feed two hundred people, the Rollers are thrown into a frenzy of excited preparations. This will be the best ever Danby Dale pie! But unfortunately, wicked Uncle Crispin, a rival pie-maker, has different plans for the Rollers' pie . . . plans that include an extra-large helping of pepper . . .

This funny, charming story was Helen Cresswell's first children's book, and was nominated for the Carnegie Medal.

Helen Cresswell was born in Nottingham and graduated in English Honours from King's College, London. *The Piemakers* was first in a distinguished series of fantasies that includes *The Nightwatchmen*, *The Bongleweed*, and *Up the Pier*, all nominated for the Carnegie Medal. She is also noted for the wickedly humorous *Bagthorpe Saga* and is a leading writer of children's television drama, twice BAFTA nominated. Series include original drama, *Lizzie Dripping* and *Moondial*, and adaptations include E. Nesbit's *The Phoenix and the Carpet* and *The Demon Headmaster* by Gillian Cross. She lives and works in a small Nottinghamshire village.

D0182596

OTHER OXFORD FICTION

The Bongleweed
Helen Cresswell

How to Survive Summer Camp
Jacqueline Wilson

Simone's Letters
Helena Pielichaty

Temmi and the Flying Bears
Stephen Elboz

Cool Clive, the coolest kid alive
Michaela Morgan

The Piemakers

Helen Cresswell

Illustrated by Tim Archbold

OXFORD
UNIVERSITY PRESS

OXFORD
UNIVERSITY PRESS

Great Clarendon Street, Oxford OX2 6DP

Oxford University Press is a department of the University of Oxford.
It furthers the University's objective of excellence in research, scholarship,
and education by publishing worldwide in

Oxford New York

Auckland Bangkok Buenos Aires
Cape Town Chennai Dar es Salaam Delhi Hong Kong Istanbul
Karachi Kolkata Kuala Lumpur Madrid Melbourne Mexico City Mumbai
Nairobi Paris São Paulo Shanghai Taipei Tokyo Toronto

Oxford is a registered trade mark of Oxford University Press
in the UK and in certain other countries

First published by Faber & Faber Ltd 1967
First published as an Oxford Children's Modern Classic 1999
First published in this paperback edition 2000

British Library Cataloguing in Publication Data available

Cover illustration by Tim Archbold

ISBN 0 19 275031 3

3 5 7 9 10 8 6 4 2

Typeset by AFS Image Setters Ltd, Glasgow

Printed in Great Britain by
Cox & Wyman Ltd, Reading, Berkshire

For my husband Brian, with love

Preface

This book is a history book, in a way. At any rate, it is based on some very old documents, and that makes it something like history.

In the attic of my great-grandmother's house I found an old box. It was cobwebby and the lock was rusty—in fact I had to take it to the locksmith to get it open at all. I broke two pairs of scissors trying to prise it open myself.

Inside the box I found several notebooks and diaries and a thick yellow wad of papers called 'The Danby Chronicles'. I sat up all night reading them, and by dawn my mind was made up. A book must be written about the piemakers of Danby Dale.

I like to think that the people this book is about are my ancestors. After all, their story was found in my great-grandmother's house, and I once made a pie myself, so it could be in my blood, handed down through the generations. I don't know how many generations, because there are no dates in the Chronicle, which made my task very much easier, because dates are inclined to confuse me.

This is the story of the Danby Dale piemakers, based on their own diaries and the Chronicle of their village.

Chapter One

Gravella Roller sat in her bedroom, writing. Her slate filled, she held it at arm's length and took a long hard look at it. She had written her own name eight times.

'Gravella Roller,' she repeated. 'Gravella Roller.'

She threw the slate down on to her patchwork quilt and herself after it. She lay with her hands under her head and stared up at the ceiling. She could still see her name written there on the white stripes between the black, lumpy beams.

'Gravella Roller.' She tried again, flourishing it on her tongue. 'I can see cobwebs on those beams. Why, oh why, Gravella? The Roller's bad enough, but Gravella!'

She knew very well why. In fact she was very lucky indeed not to have been plain Gravy. It had been her mother who had decorated it up a little, seeing that she had been a girl. She shuddered at the thought that she might have been a boy and gone through life a Gravy. Her father had been set on the name right from the start, so Jem had told her. He'd just been in the middle of making the gravy when she'd been born, and to him it was perfect.

'I suppose I should be thankful not to be a Crusty,' she told the one ambling spider who stalked his nets above her. 'Or Sagetta, or Onionana. How am I supposed to be a famous actress with a name like that? I don't even know how I've got as far in life as I have.'

'Gravella! Gravella!'

It was Jem's voice wafting up from below. She gave a great sigh and pulled herself up.

'Coming!' she called. After a pause she repeated it, 'Coming!'

She enjoyed the sound of her own voice and practised the word under her breath as she went downstairs, 'Coming, coming!'

Jem was in the kitchen, sleeves rolled up, chopping onions. The minute Gravella came through the door she could feel her eyes begin to smart.

Will I *never* get used to it? she thought with despair.

'There's another pie on the go, Gravella,' said Jem.

She was red with excitement as she always was when pies were about. Nothing else filled her with such enthusiasm, in fact when she wasn't actually 'on the go' with a pie she was rather gloomy in outlook and difficult to please.

Gravella was afraid she must have inherited this enthusiasm from Jem and Arthy. She didn't *want* to be thrilled by pies, in fact sometimes she felt as if she would scream if she ever saw another. Apart from that, a famous actress was at a disadvantage with a background of piemaking. And yet the plain truth of it was that whenever another pie was on the go she could feel her own heart treacherously thudding and her tongue aching to ask questions about it. Quite often she didn't ask questions, but that was only to save her dignity and because she knew that she would hear all about it in the end. Arthy and Jem talked pies till all hours once they were caught up in making one.

'Did you hear me, Gravella?' said Jem sharply. 'Another pie!'

Gravella groped her way to the milking stool by the chimney corner and sat down.

'I'm half-blind!' she wailed. 'Do there have to be onions?'

'Have to be onions?' Shocked, Jem laid down her knife. 'Gravella! What would your father say if he heard you!'

'Well, it could be an apple pie, couldn't it?' argued Gravella. 'It's years since we've done an apple!'

'There's no call for them,' said Jem, resuming her chopping. She chopped with enjoyment, loudly and thoroughly. Her own eyes never watered. This she put down to the fact that she kept a pressed nettle leaf in the locket that was now swinging vigorously to and fro across the front of her brown pinafore.

'It takes a big sting to chase a little sting,' she would say when people, half-blinded with tears, would comment on her own remarkable immunity. 'As my grandmother always said.'

Gravella had secret misgivings that her mother's grandmother might have been a witch. She had handed down to Jem an astonishing number of very effective charms. The only thing that reassured Gravella, who had no real wish to be descended from a witch, was that these charms and remedies only seemed to work for Jem herself. When Gravella had tried wearing a nettle leaf round her neck her eyes hadn't stopped watering until the next day, and ever since then she had refused to chop onions.

Gravella was longing to ask how big the pie was, when it was due, who had ordered it. Instead, she picked up a book from the shelf beside her and pretended to look at it.

There was only one shelf of books in the whole house and that was in the kitchen. Nobody ever read anything but recipe books. They weren't even books, in the strictest sense, because there were very few real sentences in them. Most of them were in Arthy's own laborious handwriting and contained lists of ingredients and little marginal notes that only he could understand, like 'Sage half and two tbsps and no B', or 'Crust half × quarter × four hours'.

Often Jem would read one in bed at night if she was having difficulty in dropping off and Gravella would hear her loud whispers as she woke Arthy to explain bits that she couldn't understand, or to share her excitement at some discovery.

'Arthy! Arthy! Wake up! Look! Isn't this the one we made when your Clover married the miller from Fendale? Don't you 'call it, that one where we tried the sultanas and then went and forgot the cinnamon? Oh, I'll never forget that one, not if I live to be a hundred and ten, like my grandmother did.'

This was another reason why Gravella suspected witchery. A hundred and ten, to Gravella, who was only ten and already seemed to have been alive an extremely long time, distinctly smacked of witchery.

'Gravella!'

She looked up. She knew that if she waited

long enough Jem would never be able to contain herself and would spill out the details, words headlong after each other, while Gravella tried to repress her own rising excitement.

'Guess who it's for?' Jem had stopped chopping and was scraping the onions into two earthenware bowls, ready to take out to the bakehouse where Arthy would be busy on the crust.

'I can't,' said Gravella, replacing the recipe book, since it had served its purpose now and she hadn't really had a chance to get into it. It was no use just dipping into recipe books as you could a story, they didn't mean anything if you did that. Recipes, as Arthy said, were like poems, they needed dwelling on. Sometimes on the long winter nights he would recite them, as if they were poems, and Jem and Gravella would sit rapt. Jem's cheeks would redden and she would nod vigorously as Arthy's tongue curled round the lists of ingredients and lingered over the secret combinations of herbs he loved so well.

'Gravella!' Jem's voice was sharp now. 'You're not paying attention to a word I'm saying. Now where for goodnessake did I put that bunch of sage I was drying just the other day? I could have sworn I'd hanged it just behind the door in the pantry, alonger that parsley your Uncle Crispin

6

brought us last month. Not that he come just to bring a handful of parsley, that I do know. Spying, that's all he come for, and ever is. If ever we lose our custom for pies and all go off to the workhouse we shall know where to look for a thank-you!'

Gravella realized that Jem was off on her usual track, and got up to help search for the sage. Finding it was probably the only thing that would stop her now.

'Oh! Now I've found it! Can you believe that! And I know I never put it there. I do wish Arthy would leave the herbs to me and keep to crusts and fillings!'

Gravella wandered into the pantry after her mother.

'Are those going in as well?' she asked, nodding to two sides of beef that hung from iron hooks in the ceiling.

'You don't think we're eating them for dinner, I hope,' said Jem snappishly. She sniffed the bouquet of sage, tossed her head, and marched back into the kitchen.

'I think I'll just go for a breath of fresh air,' ventured Gravella. Jem was not in the right mood for further discussion of the new pie.

'Well, mind you're back by six,' said Jem. 'It'll be a cold supper because my hands are full enough without fiddling with fancy meals.'

Gravella opened the door.

'Wait!' Jem's hand, holding a huge pair of scissors, shot into the air. 'And another thing. There's a conference tonight, so don't you be late. Mind, a conference!'

Chapter Two

Gravella pushed past the dripping laurels that bordered the path and went up the garden. Through the open door of the bakehouse she could hear Arthy singing. 'Piemaking brings out the music in me,' he said, and it was certainly true, Gravella reflected, that he sang all the time he was out in the bakehouse when a pie was on the go.

The garden at the back of the house was a tangle of weeds and the grass of the lawn merged with that of the moors beyond the fence with no noticeable difference. At one time, in a rare fit of enthusiasm, Jem had planted some foxgloves and giant sunflowers along the wall, but the only part of the garden she really took any pride in was her herb patch. This was carefully fenced off from the rest as if to protect it from the encroaching wilderness, and overlooked by a gigantic scarecrow erected 'to keep them robbing birds off', although to do the birds justice they showed very little interest in plundering that sacred patch. On fine days Jem would fetch out her rocking chair and sit by the back door contemplating her herbs for hours on end. Her eyes rarely strayed beyond them to the yellow gorse and silvery grass of the moors on to which Gravella now stepped with a half-guilty feeling of escape.

She alone of the Danby Rollers really loved the moors. Perhaps she alone of the family recognized the existence of any other world outside the sphere of piemaking. She often went for long walks, tramping in an easy rhythm over the springy turf, reciting poems that she made up as she went along. It was her enjoyment of this pastime that had made her think, lately, that she would like one day to be an actress.

She had never seen a play, but she knew that there were such things in London, and she always went to see the strolling players when they came with their wagons to the harvest supper. Even after she was supposed to be in bed she would creep up behind a hedge and watch them under the strange blend of moonlight and rushlight, tiptoe on their shadows while the bats rushed past them and the people of Danby Dale stared with pale, upturned faces.

Gravella dreamed of being an actress while knowing perfectly well that she would never be one, and not even caring very much. As long as she could dream of something she was quite happy to be a piemaker's daughter and know that she herself would follow in his steps one day.

'It's in the blood,' Arthy often said. 'Once a piemaker, always a piemaker. My father was one, my grandfather, my great-grandfather, and for all I know back to Adam and Eve. Whether Adam was one I don't know, but myself I think it very likely.'

Jem would sometimes argue about this, saying that it was going too far, but Gravella could see that she was secretly pleased to think that it might be so, and that she was proud of having married into so rich a heritage.

In a hollow under a blackthorn tree Gravella threw herself to the ground and lay there looking up at the sky. It was then that she saw the carrier pigeon.

It raced over her and raising herself on to her elbows Gravella saw that it was making straight towards her own house. As she watched it flew over the low roof of the bakehouse and into the loft.

Now I wonder what that can be? thought Gravella. She got up and started back.

But curious as she was, she could never have guessed how many unusual events were in store for her and the whole village of Danby Dale, just

because a pigeon had flown over her head and was waiting, even now, for its message to be read.

As she let herself in through the wicker gate that divided their garden from the moors, Arthy came out of the bakehouse. His tall baker's hat was at a dangerous angle and his cheeks glowed.

He's been stoking up the fires, thought Gravella, ready for the baking tomorrow.

She remembered that she didn't even know who the pie was for, let alone its size or the exact recipe.

Arthy saw her coming and waved a floury hand. He gave the impression of someone absolutely prickling with excitement.

'Has Jem told you?' he asked.

'In a way,' said Gravella guardedly. 'I know there's a pie.'

'A pie!' Arthy spread his hands and rolled up his eyes.

'Such a pie! In all your life, Gravella, you will never have seen such a one. In my life, perhaps, but in yours, never!'

'Why?' exclaimed Gravella. Her heart was thudding. 'Who's it for?'

'You won't believe me,' said Arthy. 'When the steward came I didn't believe it myself.'

'The steward!' cried Gravella. 'You don't mean . . .?'

'The Baron,' nodded Arthy. He lowered his eyes respectfully as he spoke, as if the great man himself was conjured up by the very words.

'Oh, father!' Gravella was ecstatic.

'And that's not all,' Arthy went on. 'Someone besides.'

'Who?' barely whispered Gravella.

'The King!'

The words were so reverently hushed that Gravella barely caught them. Her own blue eyes locked in stunned disbelief with Arthy's, stretched with awe.

'Oh, father!' said Gravella at last.

Arthy nodded.

'I knew that was what you'd say,' he told her. 'You see,' he lowered his voice again, 'we have never before, in the history of the Danby Rollers, baked for royalty. You know what it means, Gravella. A crest, a crest above the door, and "By Royal Appointment" in gold letters!'

Gravella knew how he was feeling. It was not just that business had been falling off lately, and that the fires had been lit only once a week for the small, family pies that Arthy secretly despised. It was the gripping adventure of making a *real* pie again, one that mattered, a pie for a hundred people, perhaps even more, a pie that had to be rolled through the street on wheels.

Arthy was blinking his eyes rapidly and rubbing them with his fists.

It was then that Gravella remembered the pigeon.

'There's a pigeon in the loft, father,' she said. 'It flew over me when I was out yonder.'

Arthy threw up his hands and almost screamed, 'The recipe! The recipe!'

His tall hat finally tottered and fell. He shrieked, clutched it, and burst into the house.

Chapter Three

For supper there was only a cold tart left over from dinner and some bread and cheese to finish with. But none of the Rollers was in a mood for eating. They ate hastily and silently and as rapidly cleared the dishes and set the rush-bottomed chairs round the scrubbed wooden table ready for the conference.

The ritual was always the same. Arthy sat at the head of the table with a large wooden spoon which he used as a hammer to control the meeting if it grew unruly. Jem always took off her pinafore, a thing she only did usually when she went to bed or there were invited callers, and pinned her grandmother's opal brooch on the front of her dress. Gravella was sent to wash her hands and brush her hair and then placed at the side of the table between Jem and Arthy.

Tonight the sense of occasion was even stronger than usual. Gravella was so nervous that she jumped when a log fell in the open hearth, showering out sparks, and she had to clench her hands tight under the table to keep them from trembling. In the light of the oil lamp placed squarely in the middle of the table, Jem's eyes looked cavernous and Arthy's red hair flickered as if he really had caught on fire with excitement and the flames were sprouting out of the top of his head.

Arthy cleared his throat.

'This conference,' he said, 'has been called to discuss—the pie.'

He paused to let the words sink in. The falling of another log made them all jump.

'The King's pie,' Arthy corrected himself.

'The King's pie,' echoed Jem in a dreamy voice. Arthy looked sharply at her.

'There's a job of work to be done,' he said, 'and until it's done, there's to be no going round with heads in the clouds dreaming of gold crests over the door and such. There isn't to be any mistakes about this pie.'

'Mistakes!' Jem threw up her hands in a gesture that would have thrown her pinafore over her face if she had been wearing it.

'There's jobs for everyone to do,' Arthy went on, 'and when they're done there'll be plenty of time for slappings on the back and going round with heads in clouds. Now, the recipe.'

Jem shot up in her chair and Gravella smelt battle.

'The recipe!' she snorted. 'You must be clear out of your mind, Arthy Roller. What's wrong with the Standard Meat with perhaps a few extra touches of herbs and more decorations on the crust? There's people in the Dale who swear by your Standard, Arthy, and to my mind it's never been bettered.'

'But, Jem,' interrupted Arthy, 'when you do a king's pie you use the king's recipe.'

'King's recipe!' Jem stabbed her finger at him. Gravella's eyes blinked rapidly from one end of the table to the other.

'How you could so lower yourself as to go crawling to that mean, nasty, underhand Crispin is right out of my understanding. And what does *he* know about king's recipes, pray? When has *he* ever baked a pie for a king?'

Confident that she had made a scoring point she sank back in her chair, the opal brooch quivering.

'It ain't a question of whether he's used it,' said Arthy patiently. 'Be reasonable, Jem, do. You can't expect Crispin to have baked for royalty any more than me—up to this present moment, that is. He was only mentioning it to me last time he was over—remember, when he dropped in with that parsley for you, Jem, and very kind of him too.'

17

'Kind! Spying, that's all that Crispin ever come here for,' retorted Jem. 'Asking questions here, poking there, prying and spying. I count them recipe books twice over when he's set foot in this house, I can tell you. The minute he's over the doorstep I get down there on my knees and count them. You're too soft, Arthy, and that's a fact. And remember, the more pies he makes, the less pies we makes. He's stealing all our eaters, and I've said so all along—'

'Jem!' pleaded Arthy.

'And that stuck-up wife of his, Essie what's her name,' Jem carried on. 'She puts him up to it, of that you *can* be sure. She's a putter-up of people if ever I saw one. The whole family was against him marrying her, and you know that's true. If I had my way—'

'Jem!' Arthy thundered. He brought the wooden spoon hard down on the table. The conference had settled into its usual pattern.

'Jem! We are using that recipe. And let there be an end to it.'

'Very well!' Jem's voice was tight and high. 'Very well, Arthy. I've had my say, and let no one say I didn't warn you. I don't like it. I don't like it at all. We should use the Standard Meat with a few extra herbs and extra trimmings on the crust. Now I've said it and I'll say no more.'

18

She pursed up her lips very tightly as if to prevent herself saying more at all costs.

Gravella herself was secretly surprised at Arthy. Knowing his pride in his old recipes and secret herb combinations, she could hardly understand herself why he should have sent a carrier straight to Uncle Crispin in Gorby Dale the minute the Baron's steward had given the order. She supposed it must be his fatal streak of kindness. He never did seem to be able to see right through Uncle Crispin as she and Jem did. He had been sorry for him because the Danby Rollers had received the order instead of the Gorby Rollers, and was trying to do him a kindness by using his king's recipe.

'Now for the jobs,' Arthy was saying. He peered short-sightedly at the slate in front of him and ran his finger down it.

'First the recipe. Gravella, you copy it out. It's that tiny on that scroll it come written on that I doubt we'll be making mistakes without. In your best hand, mind. You've had the schooling for it, which neither your mother nor me had the privilege of. As soon as the conference is over I shall give you the recipe, which I've got tucked safe in here,' he tapped the leather wallet he wore suspended from a pigskin belt, 'and you then go straight off and copy it out. On your solemn oath and honour not to repeat a word of it to a soul, mind.'

'Solemn oath and honour,' gabbled Gravella obediently. She was dizzy at the prospect of being entrusted with so vital a task.

'Now what else for you, Gravella?' muttered Arthy. 'Ah, seasonings. You did the seasonings for the Harvest Supper Steak and Kidney really beautifully, Gravella. The seasonings were very highly spoken of that night, I can tell you.'

'Oh, thank you!' breathed Gravella. The seasonings were hers! The King would eat a pie salted, peppered, and mustarded by her hand and hers alone!

'Now herbs—'

'Mine!' cried Jem, alight again, the argument over the recipe forgotten. She was like that. She flared as quick as sealing-wax and was herself again as fast.

'Yours, Jem,' agreed Arthy. 'We can always send Gravella over to Gorby for any of them you haven't—'

His voice trailed off as he saw his error.

'What did you say?' asked Jem distantly. 'What was you *about* to say, Arthy Roller?'

'I just thought,' stammered Arthy, face and hair afire together now, 'with its being a king's recipe, and us never having done it before . . .'

'I *think* I know how to grow a herb garden,' said Jem. 'I *think* I do. But *if* you don't think it good enough, I can always go straight out there and *tear* them up by the roots and *throw* them over the wall. I've *only* got a few feeble little things, *only* more than twenty different kinds which is more than you'll find in all the Dales put together and times ten!'

'Jem, now,' pleaded Arthy. 'Come on, now don't take on. Your herbs is a marvel, and aren't I always saying so? Aren't I, Gravella?'

'Oh yes,' agreed Gravella.

'A marvel,' said Arthy. 'I shouldn't even be surprised if the King remarks about them. I shouldn't be surprised if he doesn't notice them first mouthful.'

Jem reluctantly allowed herself to be mollified and Arthy went on with his list.

'Crust,' he said.

'You, of course,' said Jem.

'Yes,' said Arthy. 'But what about it? I was toying with the idea of doing a royal coat of arms as decoration with the leftovers. What do you think of that?'

'Good!' cried Jem. 'Very good indeed, Arthy. And what kind of edging'll you have? I like the dog tooth myself.'

'Mmmmm,' said Arthy. 'I did wonder about

the scallop with the raised border inside. It's fiddly, but it looks well.'

'Oh yes, do that one,' cried Gravella. 'I like that one.'

'Go on, then, do that,' said Jem graciously. 'The dog tooth is perhaps a bit bare-looking, now I think.'

'The meat I'll get up early and carve,' said Arthy. 'And then you can stew it, Jem. I'll fetch out the four iron cauldrons we put in the attic winter before last, and I'll set them up for you before I go out to the bakehouse. Because once I'm out there,' he paused, 'I don't want to be disturbed.'

'No, Arthy,' said Jem reverently.

'At six o'clock tomorrow night sharp, the pie goes in the oven.'

'Aoh, Arthy!'

'And at midnight sharp it comes out, and I taste it.'

There was silence. The three of them sat there like pillars of salt while the fire ticked and rustled. It was a moment too great for words.

Chapter Four

The Rollers were astir by dawn next day. Straight after breakfast Arthy went out and sharpened the knives and choppers ready to cut the sides of beef. While he was busy outside Gravella and Jem thoroughly cleaned and scoured the four giant black iron cauldrons which were dusty after their months up in the attic.

As they worked Jem entertained Gravella with accounts of past pies: apple, cherry, meat and gravy, but none of them, she assured Gravella, so magnificent and soul-stirring as this one.

'Just fancy!' she sighed. 'A coat of arms out of the pastry trimmings! Your father is an artist, Gravella. There's not another man in the Dales, nor in England for that matter, could work a coat of arms out of pastry trimmings. Run out to the pump, there's a good girl, and fetch another pail of water.'

Gravella took the empty pail and went to the flagstoned yard at the side of the house. She worked the handle up and down and the iron spout of the pump hesitated and then suddenly threw out a straight length of water that she caught expertly in the pail. Arthy was singing at the top of his voice as he drew the blades of his knives lovingly over the whetstone. Out on the moors the skylark was throbbing and the sun promised a glorious day that would pass unnoticed by the Rollers in their frenzy of piemaking.

'Hey, Gravella!'

She looked up, the pail now spilling on to the stones, and saw Felix the miller's boy grinning over the wall.

'Gravella! You making a pie for the King? Truly?'

'Truly,' nodded Gravella.

'How many for?' asked Felix.

'Two hundred,' said Gravella.

His face disappeared.

'Two hundred!' she heard him shout. '*Two hundred!*'

He was running down the main street into the village now, still shouting, and Gravella could hear more voices joining in. She picked up the pail and heaved it back into the kitchen.

'Just saw Felix,' she told Jem. 'He'll have told the whole village by now.'

'You'd better run up to the attic and fetch the notice,' said Jem. 'We'll be too busy for tongue-wagging this day, that I know.'

Gravella went upstairs and then mounted the wooden steps that led from the landing to the attic. There was a smell of must and faintly rotten ripeness. Apples stored from last September lay wizened under the dusty shafts of sun that streamed through the low windows. She found the notice among a pile of rusted lanterns that only came out on Hallowe'en. Dragging it after her she went back to the kitchen. A wipe with a wet rag uncovered the words 'No callers today. Pie in progress.'

'Good,' nodded Jem. 'You'd best get it up straight away before they start.'

By dinner-time the rich smell of beef stewing filled the house and drifted into the street and garden. As soon as the meal was over Arthy went out and locked himself in the bakehouse. Gravella kept walking round the kitchen touching things, fingering the bottles of herbs and jars of spices.

'Oh, for goodnessake,' snapped Jem. 'Leave off fidgeting, do, child!'

She sat at the table with the King's Recipe propped up against an earthenware jar, carefully measuring herbs and spices into tiny bowls. She kept glancing nervously at the simmering cauldrons as if half-dreading the fearful moment when the herbs must go in and spread their delicate flavours, half-tasted, half-imagined, through those rich juices.

'It's time!' She jumped up. 'Pass me the bowls, Gravella.'

One by one the bowls of greyish dust were tilted over the cauldrons. Jem, her cheeks damp and fiery, seized her largest spoon, the handle a foot long, and using both hands stirred with a look of such intensity that Gravella remembered again her mother's grandmother, and shivered.

'The seasonings!' gasped Jem, pulling up her pinafore to mop her face.

Gravella had them ready, measured and remeasured.

There looks a lot of pepper, she thought, and then, closing her eyes, dropped them in. She tried to remember the moment she had actually put them in, so that she could tell her grandchildren about it. But afterwards all she could ever remember was picking up the little blue jars and then the thunder of the cauldrons boiling filled her mind and ears, and that was all.

All afternoon the cauldrons bubbled. Jem's hair stuck to her wet face and still she stirred, running from one cauldron to the other, tending them in turn.

At four o'clock Arthy came out of the bakehouse, his eyes distant as if he were sleep-walking.

'I've done it,' was all he said.

Neither Jem nor Gravella said anything. They knew what he meant. They knew, too, that until midnight they must wait. It was a tradition of the Danby Rollers that no one but the pastry-maker should set eyes on the crust until the pie came out of the oven, though Gravella herself thought this a dangerous practice.

Arthy brought with him the wooden wheelbarrow on which, one by one, the four cauldrons were lifted and then borne out to the bakehouse. There the contents would be ladled into the huge pie-dish that had been suspended by chains from the

27

ceiling of the bakehouse for over a hundred and fifty years. Even the Danby Rollers did not make pies for two hundred eaters *every* century.

As the last cauldron sailed out into the garden Jem sat weakly on a chair and pulled her skirts up to her knees, always a gesture of extreme emotion.

'Aaaaaoh!' she gasped, like a swimmer coming up for air. 'My legs is as weak as yesterday's custard. I don't feel as if I shall ever stand again.'

'I'll fetch you a drink of milk,' offered Gravella. She went into the pantry and drew a pint of milk, and the two of them sat and sipped at it, deep in thought. They were sitting thus when the door knocker banged.

'Drat!' said Jem.

Neither of them moved. The knocker hammered again.

'Don't take a speck of notice,' said Jem. 'Haven't folks no consideration at a time like this?'

There was no further knocking.

'Aha!' came a voice from the open doorway. 'Who's been caught right out?'

Jem hastily dropped her skirts and sprang up.

'Uncle Crispin!' she exclaimed. 'Now whatever are you doing here?'

Uncle Crispin entered, rubbing his hands together. As he walked his head always seemed to be several paces ahead of his legs.

'As if,' Jem had once waspishly commented, 'those snooping eyes of his just can't wait to be in every corner at once, prying and spying!'

'Well, Jem,' said Uncle Crispin. 'What a day this must have been!'

'And still is, Crispin,' remarked Jem tartly. 'And whatever are *you* doing here?'

She repeated the question in a way that would have made Uncle Crispin very uncomfortable if he had been that kind of man.

'Family feeling,' explained Uncle Crispin, rocking backwards and forwards on his toes and heels with great energy. 'Family feeling. It's a great magnet at times like this.'

'*I'm* sure,' muttered Jem under her breath.

'And where is brother Arthy, or need I ask,' enquired Uncle Crispin jovially. 'Has he locked himself in?'

'Yes, he has,' said Jem, 'and quite right too. We don't want snooping.'

'He did use the King's recipe, didn't he?' asked Uncle Crispin. And Gravella knew by the careless way he asked that this was the real reason for the two-hour horse-ride from Gorby Dale. '*My* recipe?'

Jem was saved from answering.

'Here's Arthy,' she snapped. 'You better ask him.'

She banged out of the kitchen and could be heard wringing the handle of the pump outside with such spirit that you would have thought it was Uncle Crispin's neck.

Chapter Five

Jem had her head under the pump as Aunt Essie and Cousin Bates came through the side gate.

The first Gravella knew of their arrival was the flight of Jem through the kitchen scattering water as she went and clutching a towel to her head. Arthy and Uncle Crispin stepped deftly aside to let her pass and she was up the stairs as nimbly as a gazelle. She stopped at the top and through the folds of the towel her voice proceeded, mercifully muffled:

'*More* visitors, Arthy. *Relatives* of yours. I shall be up in my room if I'm wanted.'

As she disappeared Aunt Essie and Cousin Bates came in. Gravella was not pleased to see them, not only because she did not like them but also because they were not a particularly pretty picture.

Aunt Essie was lean and long-drawn-out as a fiddle bow and disguised herself under too many frills and ruffs and clashing bangles and rings. Her nose was so long that there was little room for anything else on her face, and her eyes in particular were darting like those of a bird. Her chin ran into her neck and both together ran into the top frill of her dress where they were fortunately lost. Aunt Essie moved her hands very delicately all the time as if she were rather gingerly feeling something that might burn her.

'Oh, Gravella, my darling,' she squealed as she advanced, 'was that your mother I saw running inside? We haven't disturbed her, I *do* hope?'

'She was cooling her head under the pump,' said Gravella. 'We're having rather a trying day, you know.'

'Oh, you poor, poor things. I *do* know,' twittered Aunt Essie. 'I knew if we came over there would be something we could do to help. And Bates was ever so eager to come, weren't you, my lamb?'

Bates growled in a very unlamblike way.

Bates had a white face, almost perfectly round, with two currants for eyes and a mouth surprisingly small for one who was eating almost as often as he was waking. Jem would often say that Uncle Crispin would never be short of trade as long as he had his own son for a customer.

'Your Uncle Crispin's come to help lay the crust on the pie, you know,' Aunt Essie confided

in Gravella. 'You couldn't expect your father to lay it single-handed.'

Gravella had not thought of this, and wondered fleetingly whether the tradition of the Danby Rollers made allowances for such occasions.

'Bates and me thought we should be able to give you and Jem a hand,' she continued. 'We've brought our things and they're in the carriage outside. Run along and fetch them, Bates dear, while I get myself settled.'

She removed her shawl, took off her bonnet, and sat in Jem's rocking chair, which she then worked with great energy. Bates returned with two large bags which he dumped on the flagstones with a great puff of relief. His tiny eyes combed the kitchen and then fastened on two slices of sultana cake that Gravella had brought out for herself and Jem before they were interrupted by Uncle Crispin's arrival.

'Are you hungry, lamb?' enquired Aunt Essie, following his gaze. 'It's a long journey, you know,' she told Gravella, 'especially for a growing boy.'

'Have some cake,' offered Gravella.

Bates took a slice in each hand and pressed it into his mouth as fast as that willing organ could admit it. Fascinated, Gravella wondered how long the pie that was in the bakehouse now would last him, and decided about a fortnight, with luck. Arthy was saying, 'I'd best go and fetch Jem and we'll all have something to eat. You must excuse her having to run up like that, but you catched her rather inconvenient with her head being under the pump, you see.'

He went to the bottom of the stairs and called up.

'Jem, Jem!'

She came slowly down. She was wearing her best shiny black dress and her grandmother's opal brooch. Her wet hair was scraped into a tight knot on top of her head and her face was very red and polished-looking as if she had rubbed it dry with the towel far longer than was necessary.

Gravella sympathized, but all the same wished Jem would carry off occasions like this with more of an air. She showed up in a bad light when she sulked, and it put Aunt Essie in the right, where she had no business to be.

'I was just saying that we'd best have a bite to eat,' said Arthy apologetically. 'What do you say, Jem?'

'Oh, quite right,' said Jem. 'It isn't Christmas, but I don't think the pantry's quite empty. I think there's a few bits of pickings there we'll make do with.'

'Good. Good, then,' said Arthy heartily. 'Me and Crispin'll just pop out to the bakehouse and get that crust laid on, and leave you ladies to have a good old gossip while you get supper.'

In the frigid silence that followed he turned and beckoned to Uncle Crispin and the two of them went out, followed by Bates.

'Well!' said Aunt Essie when they had gone. 'Well, Jem!'

'Well, Essie,' returned Jem.

There was a moment's silence and then they were off. Talking, laughing, chattering, as if they couldn't stop. It always amazed Gravella that two ladies who loathed each other as determinedly as her mother and Aunt Essie could none the less find such perverse pleasure in each other's company. Jem was rushing backwards and forwards with dishes, calling over her shoulder as she went, talking in jerks as she sawed at the bread and slapping on the butter in time with her voice, which meant a good thick spreading, Gravella saw with satisfaction. Aunt Essie, too, helped to lay the table and had a good time in the pantry lifting up lids, peering in tins and generally sniffing around.

Halfway through, when the two ladies had finished the Danby Dale gossip and were moving on to Gorby, Bates came back and stood near the table, as if for comfort.

'Are your father and uncle nearly ready, Bates?' asked Jem. 'Can I start serving?'

'Coming,' said Bates. 'Lawks, what a pie. Oh my!'

'Have you seen it?' asked Gravella, jealous. She herself had seasoned it and yet she had not had so much as a glimpse of it.

'Through the door when they went in,' said Bates. 'They wouldn't let me in. Oh my, what a pie!'

Just then Uncle Crispin and Arthy came in, very friendly and red-faced and ready to laugh at anything. By the time they were all seated round the table Gravella thought that if they were all wearing fancy hats it might as well be Christmas. She marvelled at the two-facedness of grown-ups. She and Bates disliked each other heartily and made no secret of the fact. They deliberately trod on each other's feet, told tales, and made spiteful remarks about each other. Jem and Arthy, on the other hand, put on a show of friendliness that almost deceived Gravella herself sometimes. Then, the minute the front door had closed on Uncle Crispin and Aunt Essie, they would begin abusing them and Gravella felt quite certain that the other two talked just the same about Jem and Arthy all the way back to Gorby Dale.

'That's right!' said Jem with satisfaction as the last iced bun disappeared from the plate. 'You tuck well in. I do like to see good food made good use of.'

This, Gravella well knew, would be later translated as:

'And did you *see* the way they stuffed at supper! You mark my words, that Bates'll bust before he's done. Absolutely bust. And Crispin sets him no example. Seven sausage rolls and four iced cakes, he had, as well as the pork pie and pickles, and goodness knows how many slices of bread and butter, I quite lost count. A healthy appetite's one thing, and sheer piggish gluttony is quite another.'

At any rate, supper seemed to end in a glow of good spirits and general satisfaction, and the women turned to the washing up while the two men went out to the bakehouse to put the pie in the oven.

Every now and then Jem would pause, standing with her arms up to the elbows in the sudsy water, and say wonderingly:

'It'll be in by now. Just think, at this very moment it's out there in our bakehouse, cooking.'

And Aunt Essie would say:

'Yes, and just think, if the Baron's Hall had been just a mile further on over the hill, that very pie would've been in our bakehouse at Gorby Dale at this very minute.'

And Jem, smiling, would make no comment. That, Gravella knew, would come later.

Chapter Six

Midnight seemed a long way off that evening. Bates and Gravella were promised that they could both stay up this once until the pie came out of the oven. 'History will be made,' said Jem. When the supper things were cleared and the kitchen was its scrubbed, speckless self again, bathed in the ruddy glow of the open fire, the night seemed to stretch ahead like eternity. It was almost like Christmas Eve, Gravella thought, with the same feeling of expectancy and choking impatience, and the conviction that though usually time passed, tonight it never would.

Jem set four chairs round the fire. It was quite warm, but at least the lively flickering of the flames gave them something to look at. As they all sat down and straightened their skirts Gravella gave a little giggle, as she always did if anything seemed too solemn. There was a silence. They all four sat like statues. Then Gravella, remembering Christmas, said suddenly:

'Let's all go in the parlour and play party games.'

Essie looked at her and cocked an eyebrow, then looked enquiringly at Jem. Bates said hopefully:

'With prizes?'

He's hoping there'll be slabs of cakes for prizes, Gravella thought. Jem's right, he *will* bust.

'Shall we?' she pressed.

Jem was feeling pleased with her superior position as wife of the man who was even now at this very minute baking a pie for a king. Also, she had made new curtains and cushions for the parlour since the Gorby Rollers were last over.

'Very well,' she said. 'It'll help pass the time, and we don't want to be sitting with our knees in the kitchen fire all night. Essie'll be thinking that's how we live!'

She gave a little laugh that was meant to be tinkling and amused but sounded more like a whinny. Gravella looked at her in surprise. The Danby Rollers *did* usually spend the evening with their knees in the kitchen fire, and what was wrong with that? Wisely, she said nothing.

'I'll bring the lamps,' she said.

They all rose and Jem led the way through the narrow flagstoned hall into the parlour. There was always a faint smell of must and pressed rose petals in the parlour that filled Gravella with excitement. Why it should smell of must she could not tell, because Jem dusted it every day of her life, tending it as lovingly as her herb garden itself. The dried rose petals were in little glass bowls scattered about the room 'to keep the air sweet', as Jem said.

Gravella placed one of the oil lamps on the mantelshelf and the other on the table and the room sprang into life. The corners gathered shadows. The brocade cushions gleamed softly, rose and gold. Jem edged Essie round to the tapestry chair by the fireplace from which she would have the best view of the curtains and the cushions which lay neatly along the back of the long settle.

'Sit yourself down, Essie,' she fussed. 'Gravella'll fetch a spill and put it to the fire and it'll be cosy in no time. Oh! Getting quite dark outside, I see. *Don't* the evenings draw in? I'd best draw the curtains, or we'll have half the Dale peering in at us.'

She went to the window and drew the curtains with a grand sweep. They, too, were of brocade, and she secretly stroked her rough fingers down their softness before turning back to face Essie.

'Ain't they new curtains, Jem?' she said sharply peering forwards.

'What? Oh, them!' Jem shrugged. 'Newish.'

Essie leaned back again in her chair.

'New, eh?' was all she said, but Jem did not miss the way her eyes kept darting back to them on and off during the evening.

'I'll lay my life there'll be brocade hanging in her parlour next time we're over Gorby,' she told Gravella smugly later. 'Eyes poking out like currants in a loaf all night.'

The black, carved furniture, the real Turkish rug on the floor, the pictures on the wall, all combined to give an air of festivity and occasion. They played I Spy, Hunt the Thimble, and games with slate and chalk, until even Bates was laughing and they had to stop for refreshments. Jem went out to the kitchen and Gravella helped her make a bowl of punch, steaming and fruity. They all had a tumblerful, 'Just for tasting,' and left the rest to simmer until midnight when the pie came out.

And suddenly, before Gravella could believe it possible, it was midnight. Feet scurried up the passage, and Arthy's face, red and wet, poked round the door.

'Come on, all!' he shouted. 'Pie's up!'

They jumped to their feet and hurried after him. Out through the firelit kitchen into the cold and dark of the yard and then in through the double doors of the bakehouse itself, with its warm air blowing out into the dew-drenched garden.

43

Uncle Crispin was there, wearing a borrowed cook's hat to give the impression that he, too, was an important part of the proceedings. They all pressed in, their shadows huge and swaying on the white plastered walls. The air was filled with the warm smell of pastry and simmering spices. And there, on the scrubbed trestle table, right in the middle of the bakehouse, was the pie itself. Gravella felt it was almost too much to bear.

Faintly golden, smooth and yet promising a rough, satisfying crustiness, and decorated with the Royal Coat of Arms, a slightly deeper gold, perfect as if it had been carved from stone by the chisel of a master. A little gasp ran through the huddled group. Through the hole, big as a saucer, in the middle of the pie, steam rose in a faint blue swirl.

Gravella swallowed hard and Jem distinctly sniffed and dabbed at her eyes with the pinafore that wasn't there. Arthy, spellbound as the rest, watched his creation almost as if he expected something to happen, as if it might take to the air, or a genie rise out of the steam. Suddenly he seemed to come to himself and cleared his throat to prove it.

'Well, then,' he remarked hoarsely, 'I suppose we'd better taste it.'

Bates threw back his head and sniffed like a bloodhound.

'It's beautiful!' breathed Gravella. 'Oh, it's beautiful!'

'You've certainly done that crust a treat, Arthy,' said Jem, trying hard to sound matter-of-fact, and then, giving up the attempt, burst out, 'That's the most beautiful crust I've ever seen or ever hope to live to see! I'm proud of you! Proud!'

She dabbed furiously with the invisible pinafore.

'Very nice,' nodded Essie. 'Very nice. Reminds me a bit of the one you did for Lord Cobb's funeral, Crispin. Remember, the one with the lilies worked in the middle?' But no one paid any attention. Arthy had taken a small ladle on a long handle and climbed carefully on to one of the tall stools. From this high position he leaned forward and carefully, inch by inch, lowered the ladle down through the very centre of the pie, in the faintly smoking hole. Then, carefully, he lifted it out, and gently, very gently, so as not to spill even a drop on that honey-gold crust, he brought it towards him. They all let out their breaths at once and the oil lamps flickered.

'The bowl, Gravella,' he said.

Gravella almost ran forward and picking up an

earthenware bowl from a side table held it up to her father, and he carefully emptied into it the contents of the ladle. Then he climbed down. They all drew nearer. Arthy took a soup spoon in one hand and the earthenware bowl in the other.

'Now for a taste of the King's recipe, eh, Crispin?' he said.

The spoon dipped into the gravy. He raised it to his lips, looked at them all, inclined his head slightly, and then drank. There was a second's pause and then he choked. He gasped and heaved for breath. Dropping the bowl and its contents to the floor he leaned over forwards after it and bent almost double in agony. Jem ran to him and

thumped him on the back, bang, bang, as if she were drubbing her washing. Bang, bang! Still he wheezed and tried to draw breath in huge, strained gasps. At last it was over. Slowly he straightened up, his face crimson, his eyes still gushing water. They all looked at him.

'Pepper!' he croaked at last. Just the one word—'Pepper!'

Chapter Seven

Gravella remembered turning blindly, pushing past the others and out through the half-open door, the air cold on her burning face. She remembered rushing through the empty kitchen, up the stairs and to her own room, where she flung herself on the patchwork quilt of her bed and sobbed as if her heart would break.

Her thoughts were tangled among her tears. It was all her fault. It must be. She had done the seasonings. She remembered the moment that afternoon when she had stood with the little bowl in her hand and thought fleetingly 'There looks a lot of pepper' before throwing it in. Yet she had read the recipe a hundred times and knew the quantities off by heart. Perhaps it had not been her fault. Perhaps the recipe had been wrong.

The recipe! She had copied it out last night from that minute scrap of paper that had come tied among the pigeon's feathers. She remembered how she had screwed her eyes and peered to read the writing by the dim gold light of the oil lamp on the kitchen table. It was her fault, after all. She had copied the recipe wrongly.

Among the storms of her own tears she only half knew that below her in the kitchen another storm was raging. Jem's voice, high and furious, was ordering the Gorby Rollers to take their bags and go, never to set foot in the house again.

'King's recipe!' she shrieked. 'I'll give you King's recipe, Crispin Roller! We're ruined! Ruined!'

Threaded between Jem's hysterical sobbing came Aunt Essie's indignant squeals and a thud as Jem hurled her bag, bonnet, and shawl at the kitchen door. Uncle Crispin was bawling at the two women to quieten them and Bates was just plain bawling. From Arthy there was no sound at all.

Then at last came quiet. Gravella's sobs subsided and her breath was coming in long, shaking gasps. The quilt beneath her cheek was wet and growing cold. Slowly she rose from the bed and began to go downstairs dragging her feet, unwilling to reach the bottom.

In the kitchen Arthy and Jem sat each at one end of the table, their heads buried in their hands. Still simmering at the hob was the bowl of fruity punch that was to have been the glory of their celebrations.

Gravella stood still by the door and Jem looked up and saw her.

'Come along, child,' she said. 'Get by the fire where it's warm.'

Gravella walked slowly to the fire and sat on the milking stool, clasping her arms round her knees for comfort. Arthy still had not raised his head.

'I'm sorry, I'm sorry! It's all my fault!' she cried suddenly, and jumped up and ran to Jem, who held her tightly against the shiny black dress with its tiny pricking beads and smell of lavender.

'There, there!' said Jem soothingly. 'No one's blaming you, child.'

'I put the pepper in,' sobbed Gravella, her voice smothered in the warm folds of the dress.

'You put it in,' said Jem grimly. 'But whose recipe told you to put it in?'

Gravella went on. She could not bear her guilt alone.

'But I copied out the recipe!' she cried. 'I must have copied it out wrong. And now we shall never know, because I threw the scrap of paper away, in the fire!'

There was a little pause. Not a very long one, but long enough for Gravella to feel that Jem was beginning to have her doubts.

'Fiddlesticks!' snapped Jem then. 'No such thing, and don't let me hear of it again. All along I knew that King's recipe of that creeping Crispin'd be no good to us. Done it o'purpose, of course. Jealousy, that's at the bottom of it all. Crispin's never been able to forgive your father for being a better piemaker than he is or could ever be, and this is how he serves us!'

'Now, Jem, that's not fair.' It was Arthy. At last he had raised his head and Gravella saw that the red, shining face of half an hour ago was almost white now, and pinched-looking, as if grief had shrunk it as frost shrinks blossom.

'Arthy Roller,' said Jem, 'you know that every word I'm saying's the truth. You and your family loyalty! Look where it's got us now. If you hadn't been so—so *stupid* kind-hearted and so downright *ridiculous* generous, all this would never have happened.'

'Now, Jem,' said Arthy again. 'There isn't a scrap of use in going over it all. The fault's not to be laid at anyone's door. The thing is—what's to do now?'

'Yes,' said Jem. 'What is?'

'What is?' echoed Gravella, for the first time really thinking what the spoilt pie meant. It was a pie for a king, and it was uneatable.

'Will we be put in prison?' she cried. 'Will we?'

'Don't be silly,' said Jem sharply. 'Prison indeed! You don't go to prison for spoiling pies, king or no king. Not that there aren't some people I can think of who'd be rightly served by being sent there. It'd be Essie that put him up to it, of course. She's the one who does all the putting up.'

'We shall have to think of something,' said Arthy. 'No one must ever know what really happened.'

'Why not?' asked Gravella wonderingly. 'No one will blame you, father. It was only a mistake.'

'The Danby Rollers don't make mistakes,' said Arthy. 'Leastways, they have never been known to.' His voice was suddenly alive again and his back had straightened. 'The honour of the Danby Rollers rests on that pie out there, and I'm not going to be the man to ruin it.'

'What's the way out?' asked Jem in despair. 'Oh, Arthy, I know how you feel. My heart bleeds, it fairly bleeds. But the steward'll be here at dawn with his men and the wagon to fetch it and there's no time to bake another. Not if we had fifty pairs of hands apiece, there isn't.'

'No,' said Arthy, 'there is no time to bake another.'

'Then what?' demanded Jem. 'What can we do?'

Arthy got up slowly.

'You and Gravella go to bed now,' he said. 'Leave it to me.'

Jem stared up at him.

'Go to bed?' she said incredulously. 'At a time like this? I could no more go to sleep than I could ride a broomstick.'

Gravella shuddered. Why must Jem always be reminding her of her great-grandmother?

'You needn't go to sleep,' said Arthy. 'Just go to bed. Both of you.'

It sounded like a command. Arthy very rarely gave anyone a command and they were so surprised that they were halfway up the stairs before they realized what they were doing. Jem paused and threw out her arms in an imploring gesture.

'Arthy, what are you going to do? Let me help.'

'Go to bed,' was all he said.

Gravella undressed quickly and hurried under the blankets, clutching a rag doll that she was far too old to play with but that was comforting at a time like this. She heard her father go out of the kitchen across the cobbled yard and into the bakehouse.

For a long time she lay staring up at the little square of sky above her on the sloping ceiling. Whether she fell asleep or not she did not know, but all of a sudden there was a lot of noise, voices shouting and even screams. She jumped up and ran to the window.

The bakehouse was on fire. The flames were already curling out of the door and windows and licking along the wooden beams of the roof. Around it in the black night it shed a golden halo, every leaf and blade of grass was lit up and even the fringes of the moor itself. Jem's scarecrow writhed as its shadow danced with the flames.

She saw Jem rush out beneath her, her hair flying behind her in two long plaits. And Arthy, brave, undaunted Arthy, was running up and down the garden wringing his hands and tugging at his orange hair and shouting:

'My pie! My pie! Help, everyone. My pie's in there, my pie for the King!'

Even in the midst of her grief and terror Gravella thought:

No wonder I want to be an actress—I get it from father.

He darted to the blazing door of the bakehouse and three onlookers ran forward to drag him back as he kicked and struggled and his cry of anguish seemed to rise and mingle with the long flames that were spearing now through the very roof of the bakehouse.

'My pie! My pie!'

At that moment, the roof fell in. The honour of the Danby Rollers had been saved.

Chapter Eight

The days that followed the burning of the bakehouse were as grey and cheerless as the heap of ashes that still lay in the garden outside the back door. No more was Arthy's voice to be heard as he sang the entries and exits of pies in and out of the ovens. Instead he loafed about the house.

'For all the world like a duck without a quack,' as Jem picturesquely put it.

He seemed in no hurry to rebuild the bakehouse.

'I think I'm finished with pies,' he would say whenever Jem brought the subject up. 'I just haven't got the heart for them any more.'

'Fiddlesticks!' Jem would retort. 'You're the best piemaker in the Dales. If you don't start making pies again soon, that Crispin'll take all your trade. Just what he wanted, I shouldn't wonder. I daresay he had a very good laugh indeed when he heard the bakehouse was burnt to nothing. I shouldn't mind going over to Gorby one dark night myself and setting fire to his bakehouse.'

'Now, Jem,' said Arthy, alarmed. 'There's no need for that kind of talk.'

'Tell me what we're going to do, then,' said Jem. 'If you don't start making pies again soon we shall all be in the workhouse by Christmas.'

'I've got a bit put by,' said Arthy. 'There's no call to go exaggerating.'

'We're not spending our savings,' said Jem with decision. 'Them's for emergencies, and nothing else.'

'This *is* an emergency,' pointed out Arthy.

'It needn't be, though,' retorted Jem. 'Not if you was to get down to things like a man and get baking pies again. It'd take you out of yourself a bit. You've had long enough now spooning about weeping and wailing over that dratted pie. What's done's done. Best forget all about it and start where you left off.'

'It's not the kind of thing you can forget,' said Arthy. 'It's taken all the heart out of me.'

At the end of a conversation such as this Jem would cluck loudly and bang the pots and pans furiously about the kitchen until Arthy, unable to stand it any longer, would sidle out into the garden and stand wistfully surveying the pile of ashes where once his joy had been.

Gravella herself grew pale and quiet, partly because she felt as if she herself was to blame, whatever anyone said to the contrary, and partly because seeing Arthy so unhappy made her unhappy too.

The saving of them all came out of the blue, just as their ruin had on the pigeon's back. One afternoon Jem was shelling peas in the kitchen while Arthy sat thumbing half-heartedly through some of his recipe books. Gravella was out in the yard, swinging on the gate.

As she swung to and fro, bending her head right back to look into the dim green heart of the elm above her, she heard the clatter of horses' hooves. She jerked her head back up and blinking a little with dizziness was just in time to see three men riding abreast past the house. They wore red and gold livery and the one in the middle carried a long golden trumpet from which hung an emblazoned banner. Gravella recognized the coat of arms even in that brief glimpse. She jumped from the gate and was past the pump and in at the kitchen door in only half a dozen bounds.

'The King's messenger!' she cried. 'They're here. Oh, mother, have they come for us?'

'Don't talk nonsense,' said Jem. 'All that was over long ago. King's messengers? Where are they now?'

'I don't know,' said Gravella. 'They just rode past down to the village. Shall I go and look?'

'Yes,' said Jem. 'Go and have a look. You'd best run.'

Obediently Gravella ran through the gate and down the street to the village. She could see below her the stone cross on the green and the three messengers halted by it. People were already gathering round and as Gravella ran she could hear the call of the trumpet. Panting for breath she arrived on the green just in time to see the herald take a long scroll with a huge golden seal and, unrolling it, begin to read:

'By Royal Proclamation ye are hereby notified on this fourteenth day of April that His Majesty the King being desirous of supping on a pie of the Dales, and that the best to be found, is holding a Grand Contest. To the Piemaker of the Dales who shall by the third day of June make a pie the biggest and best by common consent, shall go a purse of One Hundred Guineas, and the right to carry above his door the Royal Coat of Arms signifying appointment by His Majesty the King.'

A murmur of excitement ran through the crowd and Gravella saw people nudge each other and look at her. But she did not wait. Up the street she sped again, almost as fast as she had gone down, until gasping for breath she ran again through the kitchen door.

'Oh, father, mother!' she panted. 'Wait till you hear!'

'Come on, then,' said Jem. 'Hear what?'

'A contest!' gasped Gravella. 'For a pie!'

'A contest!' ejaculated Jem.

'The biggest and best pie in the Dales. A prize of a hundred guineas—think, a hundred guineas—and the King's coat of arms above the door!'

'For goodnessake!' Jem sat down suddenly as if her legs had folded like hinges of their own accord. 'A hundred guineas! Did you hear that, Arthy?'

Arthy was staring at Gravella as if the words had not really yet sunk in.

'Just think,' cried Gravella. 'He could build the bakehouse up again even better than before!'

'Wait!' said Jem. 'How are we going to bake a pie in the first place if we haven't a bakehouse? And where's the money coming from?'

'The savings?' suggested Gravella.

'Them's for emergencies,' said Jem with finality.

All three of them remained silent, deep in thought.

'We'll think about it,' said Jem at last. 'Won't we, Arthy?'

'We'll think about it,' said Arthy. 'But I don't see what we can do about it.'

'Now then!' said Jem sharply. 'None of that gloomy, despairing talk. This is what you've been waiting for, Arthy Roller, to set you up on your feet again where you belong. And this time there'll be no Kings' recipes from Gorby to spoil your chances. It'll be a Danby Dale Standard Meat with extra trimmings, or it'll be over my dead body.'

'The way you talk all I've got to do is walk out there and put it in the oven,' said Arthy. 'Except there isn't even an oven to put it in.'

'There will be,' said Jem. 'Straight after supper we'll have a conference. That's what we'll do. We'll have a conference, and we'll work out what's to be done.'

'A conference?' Arthy's face brightened in spite of himself. 'Yes, we could do that, Jem.'

And as for Gravella, she had no doubts at all that a conference, as usual, would solve everything.

Chapter Nine

By half past seven the supper things were cleared, Jem had taken off her pinafore and put on her opal brooch, and all three of them were sitting straight-backed at the table. There was that special air of excitement and occasion that a conference always brought, and Gravella, staring at the opal brooch, wondered whether that had anything to do with the magic of conferences. It had, after all, almost certainly been worn by one who had almost certainly been a witch.

Arthy had just cleared his throat when there was a loud knock on the front door.

'Would you believe it?' said Jem. 'At a time like this!'

The knock came again.

'I suppose we'd better see who it is?' suggested Arthy. 'It might be important.'

'It might!' sniffed Jem. 'It might be another pigeon from Gorby, can't find its way into the loft. I'll go.'

She stamped out and though Arthy and Gravella strained their ears they could not catch any of the conversation at the door. The first thing they heard clearly was footsteps coming up the passage. Gravella and Arthy made surprised faces at each other. There were more than one person's footsteps.

Jem led the way into the kitchen followed by Ned Bantam, the village blacksmith, and Farmer Leary.

'Well then, gentlemen,' said Jem, rather huffily. 'Here he is, and perhaps you'll have your little word with him and be away, if you'll be so kind. I told them we were just starting a conference,' she explained to Arthy, 'but for some reason they thought it a good time to interrupt.'

Arthy got to his feet looking rather awkward and shamefaced.

'Good evening to you,' he said, holding out his hand. 'It'll be some time since I saw you last.'

'Ay, Arthy, a bit ago, I believe,' agreed the blacksmith, swallowing Arthy's hand with his own. Gravella, watching them, noticed that the top of Arthy's head just reached the next to the top button on the blacksmith's leather jerkin.

'You too,' said Arthy, shaking hands with the farmer in turn. He had not once been down to the village since the night of the fire, and even people who had called at the house to bring their sympathy had seen only Jem. Gravella could understand this. It would be hard to take sympathy from people for a fire you had started yourself.

'You're lucky, Mistress Roller,' said Ned, addressing himself to Jem, 'that you haven't the trampling feet of the whole of the Dale in your kitchen tonight.'

'Oh indeed?' said Jem. 'And for what, pray?'

'They were all wanting to come, I assure you,' nodded Farmer Leary. 'But they picked us out to come for them. I told them you wouldn't want everyone.'

'I should think not,' said Jem. 'And what was it you said you'd come about?'

'We didn't say,' said Ned. 'We're just about to be going to.'

'Just going to,' agreed Farmer Leary.

'Go on, then,' invited Jem. 'You'd best sit down first.'

So they both sat and both held their caps in their hands between their knees, and the blacksmith began.

'It's about this contest,' he began. 'You'll have heard about it?'

'We've heard,' said Jem.

'And the truth of it is,' went on the blacksmith,

'that we in Danby think you're the man to win that contest, Arthy Roller.'

'Well!' said Jem, pleased.

'And we mean to see you do,' said Ned.

'Every man Jack of us,' nodded Farmer Leary.

'You see, we thought this thing over after them heralds had blown away,' the blacksmith said, 'and the words of that notice was very clear. "Biggest and best." D'ye see? "Biggest and best".'

'Well?' said Jem. 'What of it?'

'It's the "biggest" we've come about,' said Ned. 'You see, the way we look at it is this. There isn't one scrap of doubt but what Arthy here can bake the *best* pie in the Dales. Now ain't that right?'

'Right,' said Jem and Farmer Leary together.

'But the notice said the pie was to be judged by "common consent". Now parson says that means all the people there will be the judges. Now, if there's more men from Gorby, say, or Crandock Dale, it stands to sense they'll put their word in for their pie.'

'True enough,' put in Jem, who was listening intently now, plucking her opal brooch and leaning right forward in her chair.

'So the way to make right sure that Arthy here's the rightful winner,' went on Ned triumphantly, 'is for his to be the biggest.'

There was another silence. Arthy cleared his throat.

'So you think I should bake a really big one, then,' he said uncertainly. 'Two hundred, say?'

'Thousand,' said Ned.

There was an enormous silence. Gravella could hear her own heart beating. They all sat there like so many dumb stones.

'*Pardon?*' said Jem loudly at last.

'*Two thousand,*' said Ned. 'That's how big.'

Gravella looked at Arthy. His face was beginning to burn and his red hair to sprout flames. He got up from his chair and began to pace up and down the kitchen.

'Thousand,' he muttered, 'two thousand.'

He suddenly whirled round to face the others.

'It can't be done!' he shouted. 'It can't be done!'

And from the way he said it Gravella knew that his mind was already furiously searching for ways and means that it could be done, and would find no rest till it was. Arthy Roller was on fire again.

'The whole of the Dale's behind you, Arthy,' said Farmer Leary. 'Remember that. You've only got to speak for what you need, and it'll be got for you.'

'But it'll be the biggest pie that's ever been made in the whole history of the world!' Arthy almost screamed. He was fairly dancing now, twitching with excitement and a kind of wild joy. Jem, on the other hand, was for once quite at a loss. She merely sat, trying to take things in, without so much as a word to say for herself.

'Two thousand!' Arthy shrieked again, and again, just to get the feel of it. 'Two thousand!'

Farmer Leary and the blacksmith sat and watched him with pleased faces. Gravella wanted to hug them both but instead just smiled back at them and watched Arthy kindling himself.

'It'll have to be worked out,' said Arthy. 'The whole thing, from beginning to end. I can do it, I know I can.'

'Of course you can, Arthy,' said Ned. 'You just think it over and have your conference and let us know what's to be done. Me'n Leary'll be off now that we've had our say.'

'Thank you, thank you!' cried Arthy. He seized their hands and wrung them again and again.

'And remember, Arthy,' said Farmer Leary, 'every man in the Dale's at your command.'

'Oh!' cried Arthy. 'It's too much!'

Jem, still dazed, followed them into the corridor. When the front door had closed behind them she came back and sat down heavily again, shaking her head.

'I ain't a-dreaming, am I?' she asked. 'We ain't *all* dropped off and a-dreaming?'

'No, Jem,' said Arthy. 'We ain't dreaming.'

'They said two thousand, and you said you'd do it?'

'That's it,' said Arthy. He winked at Gravella and started to tug his orange hair as if trying to pull ideas out of his head by force.

'Well, I'll be gobberguckled!' said Jem—'as my grandmother used to say.'

Chapter Ten

The Great Pie took root in the hearts and minds of Danby Dalesmen. Within two or three days of its first being thought of, everyone in the Dale lived, talked, ate, and slept pies with a fanatical fervour that until now had been confined to the Roller family.

It was agreed that to ensure the success of their plan the utmost secrecy was necessary. It was particularly important, as Jem said, that Gorby Dale should have no hint of what was going on. She explained this publicly by saying that as Crispin was also a Roller, it followed that he would be Arthy's closest rival. Her private reasons were, of course, very different, and were aired thoroughly and frequently for Arthy's and Gravella's benefit.

'If he so much as sniffs what we're up to,' she said, 'he'll find some way to pull us down. We've go to be that secret we hardly know what we're doing ourselves.'

The people of the Dale, Gravella knew, were

well aware of the rivalry between the Gorby and the Danby Rollers. Some of them might even have had their suspicions as to the fate of the King's Pie. At any rate, they all put loyalty to the Pie and the Dale before everything else, and at once stopped all visits to relatives and friends in other dales. It was not so easy, though, Ned Bantam pointed out, to prevent other people from visiting Danby.

'We can't go locking ourselves in for the next two months,' he said, 'so there's only one thing for it. We must hide the pie.'

His idea was that anyone visiting Danby would naturally think that Arthy, whose fame was widespread, would be baking a pie to represent his Dale.

'It ain't no good, then,' he pointed out, 'going building up your bakehouse again specially for this pie. We'd have to build it that enormous that it'd make people gawp, and the game would be up. No, we'll all get together and build a bakehouse natural—just like it was. And then there'll be nothing to draw people's notice, like.'

'And where will the real pie be?' demanded Arthy.

'In my barn,' Farmer Leary told him. 'That's where it'll be. Where they'd no sooner think of looking than under a toadstool.'

It was generally agreed that the idea was sound. It appealed particularly to Jem.

'That creeping Crispin'll be over here before long, snooping and spying,' she said. 'He'll be creeping over the moors and in at the back garden and peering in the bakehouse when folks are fast asleep in their beds. We'll get a big dog, that's what we'll do, and tie him to the bakehouse door. A good one with teeth that'll fetch his leg off if he tries his tricks.'

For nearly a week, then, the men in the village were working on the rebuilding of the bakehouse. Sometimes fifteen or twenty of them were there at once, and Jem would be kept running backwards and forwards with food and drink, grumbling and hugely delighted. On the seventh day the work was completed. On the eighth day Jem went straight out after dinner and came home two hours later with the Dog.

'What've you got there, Jem?' ejaculated Arthy when he saw it. He dropped rapidly back several paces.

'Dog,' said Jem briefly.

'Are you sure?' said Arthy. 'It looks a little like a wolf to me, Jem. You're sure, now?'

'Of course,' said Jem. 'The more it looks like a wolf and the more it acts like one the better pleased I'll be. I got it from the gypsies.'

Arthy dropped back even further. Gravella stood her ground, because fierce and enormous as the animal seemed, she thought its eyes were gentle, even a little frightened.

'If it's come from the gypsies it *is* a wolf,' said Arthy with decision. 'Best take it straight back, Jem. Mind how you go, and watch it doesn't bite you. I'd go with you myself only I said I'd meet Ned and Leary down at the village.'

Jem laughed and let the dog off the long chain she held.

'Clever as a fox, with the roar of a lion and the heart of a lamb,' she said.

And so it turned out to be. Within two days Arthy was not to be seen anywhere about the village without Dog at his heels, and at last Gravella had a companion for her tramps across the moors.

Jem refused to give the animal any other name besides 'Dog'.

'Give an animal a name and you give it a soul,' she said. 'That's what my grandmother used to say. She had a cat, and as long as she lived I never heard her call it any other name but Cat.'

'What colour was the cat?' asked Gravella. She didn't want to ask, but felt forced to.

'What colour?' asked Jem staring. 'What's that to do with it?'

'I just wondered,' said Gravella, half-thankful not to know for certain.

'Well, if you must know, it was black,' said Jem. 'And she didn't call it Sooty or Jet or any of that nonsense. Just plain Cat.'

And it seemed more clear than ever to poor Gravella that her great-grandmother had been just plain Witch.

Just plain Dog slept in the garden and during the night he would sometimes wake and bay to the moon under Gravella's window, waiting for Uncle Crispin to come creeping.

As soon as Arthy's bakehouse had been rebuilt

the really important task of converting Farmer Leary's barn into a bakehouse was next to be tackled. Arthy drew all kinds of plans and pictures to demonstrate how he wanted it to be. He drew on slates, on walls, on stone floors, and even, to Jem's annoyance, on tables.

'I can't see why there's got to be all this doodling and drawing,' she said. 'All you want's an oven big enough to get the pie-dish in and a good-size table for pastry-making. It don't take a deal of doodling and drawing to work that out.'

'Making a pie for two thousand eaters ain't as easy as you make out, Jem,' Arthy said with dignity. He went on drawing. At last the plans were drawn up to his satisfaction and work inside the barn began. Eight men in the village worked in shifts to build the ovens and make the necessary tables. There were always two scouts posted at each end of Farmer Leary's ten acre in which the barn stood. If strangers approached, they gave a signal and all hammering and banging in the barn stopped until the signal was given that danger had passed.

'Gives the job a bit of spice, like,' commented Cedric Winter, the carpenter. 'I can feel my spine fair tingle when that whistle goes.' And this summed up very well the whole atmosphere of Danby Dale during those busy days of building and rebuilding, when the very foundations of the Great Pie were being laid. The mixture of excitement and secrecy made Spy Hunting so fashionable a sport that a password was even invented to be given by everyone entering the ten acre, despite the fact that everyone in the Dale had known everyone else since childhood. When Gravella pointed this out, Arthy, usually the most reasonable of men, said darkly:

'There's such a thing as disguises, Gravella. You just can't be too careful on a thing like this.'

Jem added, 'Folks as come snooping and spying is sharp, Gravella, and I don't want to hear of that creeping Crispin sneaking into that barn disguised as *anybody*.'

So the password remained. Gravella was not nearly so much interested in the activity inside the barn as in the actual details of the pie itself, and could hardly wait for the real making to begin. And just three weeks after the visit of the King's messengers, it did begin.

Chapter Eleven

'The dish,' said Arthy, 'that's the main thing. The rest's up to me, but I can't begin to bake a pie for two thousand without a dish big enough to put it in. And that stands to reason.'

A conference was being held in the Roller kitchen, and Arthy was making his opening speech. This was not a real Roller conference in the sense that all its members were not 'family'. Farmer Leary and Ned were both there, and so was Miller. Miller's real name was Bob Bedlow, but everyone in the Dale had forgotten this long ago, including himself. Everyone called him Miller, just as they called Parson Parson and Doctor Doctor. They told a story in the Dale that a stranger had one day knocked at the door of the mill asking for Bob Bedlow. The miller's wife, who had opened the door, replied that she had lived in the Dale for over thirty years and knew no one of that name, and had sent him away. Gravella thought the story a little far-fetched, but enjoyed it just the same.

'As to that dish,' Ned said. 'That's something I can settle. My brother Jarge, who lives up Wedbury, he can make it, for I've asked him.'

'Wedbury!' ejaculated Jem. 'But that's eight miles away. And the road between here and there's as up and down as a camel's back and twice as awkward.'

'Aye,' chipped in Arthy. 'And you've to come through Gorby to get from there to here. We should never get it here in secret, Ned, and that's a fact.'

'No,' agreed Ned, 'we shouldn't. And we ain't.'

'Ain't?' repeated Arthy, puzzled.

'Ain't,' said Ned. 'We shall bring it down the river.'

Everyone sat taking in this amazing statement.

'We shall float it down the river as if it was a boat,' said Ned. 'We shall steer it down with poles.'

'I never heard the like!' cried Jem. 'Float a pie-dish down the river, like as if it was a boat! Oh my!'

She started to laugh, but seeing Ned look rather offended stopped as abruptly as she began, so that all she really let out was a kind of squark, like a hen's.

'Amazing!' Arthy was shaking his head in wonder. 'Truly amazing! *That's* something that's never happened before in the history of the Rollers. *That*'ll make history.'

'So what do you say?' asked Ned.

'I say if it can be done, then that's the way to do it,' said Arthy. 'And a slap on the back for you, Ned, for hitting on the idea.'

'If you ask me,' said Jem, who had recovered from her amazement and was her old sharp self again, 'there'll be more folks staring at a pie-dish come floating down the river than there would at one coming up the road!'

'Ah, but the river Dan don't flow through Gorby, Jem,' pointed out Arthy, 'nor through any village, for that matter.'

'And we can disguise it,' cried Gravella, delighted by the whole idea. 'We can disguise it as a boat, can't we, father?'

'In any case,' said Arthy, 'if anyone does chance to see it, the last thing they'll think they're looking at is a pie-dish. Who would ever think of seeing a pie-dish on a river?'

And this closed the argument. It was settled that Jarge should start making the pie-dish straight away, and that it should be floated down the river from Wedbury to Danby Dale.

'Now as to flour,' went on Arthy then. 'That's up to you, Miller.'

Miller beamed hugely.

'I never thought I should live to grind the flour to make the pastry to cover the pie a king will eat,' he said.

This was exactly what he had said when Arthy had ordered the flour for the first, fateful pie, and Gravella hoped that this time he would not be disappointed.

'You'll be needing a fair amount,' he said.

'Fairish,' agreed Arthy. 'More than a cupful.'

'Best quality. In fact, better than best quality, if possible, seeing it's for the King.'

'We know we can rely on you, Miller,' said Jem flatteringly. Miller had a reputation for talkativeness and would ramble on all night if left to himself. 'Shall we say we'll leave it all up to you?'

That, too, was settled. So was the number of cattle that would be needed for the meat and gravy. This conference, Gravella reflected, was much more smooth-running than the ones confined to the Roller family. No one had shown so much as a sign of going off into a huff, and the opal brooch was having a very quiet night of it.

Jem got up and brought in the supper and after hot mince pies and candies the three visitors went home. Jem, Arthy, and Gravella sat on round the table.

'It'll be Standard Meat, of course,' said Jem in an offhand way, adding, 'with trimmings.'

Gravella held her breath.

'It'll be an honest to goodness Roller Standard Meat, Jem,' said Arthy. 'With or without trimmings, that's the pie I'll stand or fall by.'

'Oh, Arthy!' cried Jem, quite overcome by the unexpectedness of her victory. 'I hoped you'd say that.'

'I shall do the coat of arms with the pastry trimmings just the same,' Arthy went on. 'It should be even better than last time, with having had a practice like.'

'Oh Arthy!' breathed Jem.

Her happiness was completed that night when at three o'clock the whole family was woken by the sound of Dog growling furiously and human yells of pain and terror. Gravella jumped out of bed and ran on to the landing, where she met Jem, plaits whirling and a meat axe in her hand. (Jem had taken to sleeping with a meat axe by her bed along with her Bible.)

'It's Crispin!' she hissed. 'Dog's got Crispin!'

Arthy came scurrying up behind, rubbing his eyes and protesting:

'Now you wait, Jem. Leave it up to me. Robbers is a man's job.'

But Jem was already descending the stairs, the axe raised high.

'Jem!' shouted Arthy, his hair crackling now

with alarm. He leapt down the stairs after her, two at a time, and Gravella followed as fast.

At the back door the procession was halted while Jem began to draw the extra bolts and catches and turn the keys she had made Arthy put on. She fumbled and bodged them in her haste, muttering furiously all the while under her breath. Arthy was capering round her uttering shouts of protest and warning, and so great was the commotion indoors that it was not until Jem had triumphantly shot back the last bolt and flung open the door that they realized that outside there was perfect quiet.

They stood, all three of them listening intently. Gravella could hear the soft sough of the wind through the dry moor grass, and the faint creaking of the herb garden scarecrow. As her eyes grew accustomed to the moonlight she could see the vast, whitish sea of the moors beyond the garden fence, and then Dog, advancing through the silvered weeds, his tail erect and stiff.

'Dog! Come here!' commanded Jem.

Dog obeyed, and then they saw that he had something in his mouth. Jem snatched it up and held it out with a cry.

'Look! What did I tell you! Dog's got a bit of Crispin's jerkin!'

Arthy peered forward to see the piece of cloth that Jem was dangling out. The axe, forgotten, she dropped to the ground.

'It's a bit of jerkin, all right,' agreed Arthy, 'but I can't rightly say that it's Crispin's, Jem, I don't recall—'

'Would you believe it!' snorted Jem in disgust. She turned and stamped back into the kitchen. 'Some folks can't see things as plain as the nose on their faces. That's a bit of cloth off that spying, creeping Crispin, and no one's going to tell me different. If it hadn't been for Dog, he'd have been in that bakehouse, peering and prying and ferreting round and never a soul to know. I *knew* that Crispin'd be creeping before long!'

And so she went to bed, thoroughly happy, and the next day made one of her grandmother's spells and dropped the piece of cloth into it.

'That'll settle Crispin,' she said.

And certainly Dog did not bark in the night again. But that, Gravella reflected, was not necessarily witchery. Once bit, twice shy, she thought. More likely that than witchery. The thought comforted even if it did not quite convince her.

Chapter Twelve

On May 11th ten stout Danby Dalesmen and Gravella went to Wedbury to fetch the pie-dish. It was a hot, brilliant day with a copper sun, and all the way they sang songs as they rolled between the hedges and out on to the bare white road over the moors.

Jarge's smithy, as luck would have it, was on the outskirts of Wedbury, and right on the very bank of the River Dan. It was a high, grey stone building, screened by tall elms, and the very place for the secret launching of a pie-dish.

Jarge himself was a giant of a man half a head taller than Ned himself, and he had a mane of flaxen hair and, very oddly, a flaming red beard. This intrigued Gravella so much that she found it very hard not to stare and had to keep deliberately pulling her eyes away and staring hard at something else.

The ten Dalesmen trooped into the forge at Jarge's invitation and found ten large tankards of cool gleaming ale, and ten huge slices of

Wedbury pie, all lined up on a low trestle table. As they gulped their eyes grew enormous above the rims of their tankards when they first made out in the shadowy light the pie-dish, almost filling the forge.

'The tales I've telled over that dish,' said Jarge happily, accepting the slaps on the back and wringings of the hand. 'Do you know what I told folks it was? I said it was a fish pond!'

He laughed very loudly, throwing back his head to enjoy it.

'But it don't *look* like a fish pond, Jarge,' said Arthy anxiously. 'D'ye think folks believed you?'

'If you was to dig a big hole and put that dish in it, it'd make as good a fish pond as you'd ever find,' said Jarge. 'And as to if they believed me, who cares? No one ever mentioned to me as they thought it might be a pie-dish, and I should think not, indeed! Who ever heard of a pie-dish that size? I'll tell the truth, and say it looks more like a fish pond than a pie-dish to *me*, and I made it!'

He laughed again and then lifted his tankard and rinsed his mirth down in a long, noisy gulp.

'Now!' he said. 'What about launching?'

The ten Dalesmen put down their tankards and straightened their shoulders.

'Ready, Jarge,' nodded Ned. The Dalesmen ranged themselves round the pie-dish.

'What's this?' said Arthy, pointing. 'What's this say?'

Gravella saw that near the rim of the pie-dish, in bright red paint, were the words, 'The Jolly Dan'.

Jarge blushed modestly.

'Just a thought of mine,' he said. 'To disguise it, make it look more like a boat.'

'Well, I hope the paint comes off,' said Arthy dubiously, then adding, 'Good idea, though, Jarge. That brother of yours has got a head on his shoulders, Ned.'

Jarge's face threatened to match his beard.

'I don't believe I am a fool,' he agreed, 'or I shouldn't have thought of it, should I?'

Then came the launching. The pie-dish was on a very low wooden trolley so that it could be guided through the double doors of the forge and over the strip of grass to the river's edge. Four men stood at each side and one at each end, and the work of pushing began, among shouts of 'Steady now,' and 'Mind the post!' and 'Hold her!' Gravella ran up and down and round and round the pie-dish, jumping anxiously when it struck a pile of old horse-shoes and letting out a shriek of delight and excitement as the edge was carefully lowered down over the bank.

She looked at the red, shining faces of the Dalesmen and saw the sun shafting down among the elms to strike fire from the sides of the dish, and thought, This is history. This isn't just Roller history, it's real history.

With a final, graceful lunge the pie-dish slipped into the water and lay rocking gently there as comfortably as a barge. It looked so at home among the long, pale green trailers of the willows and the brown moorhen and her

brood, that it seemed to Gravella that this pie-dish had been meant to sail, right from the start, had been *born* to it, almost.

'There! What a beauty!' cried Leary, and the rest of the Dalesmen let out a cheer.

There were holes drilled in the rim of the pie-dish from which trailed ropes. These were made fast to a nearby tree and everyone stood arms akimbo for a few minutes to stare in pure delight at the bobbing pie-dish.

'Now then,' said Jarge at last. 'This won't do.

We can't keep that dish there for long. Who's sailing?'

Arthy, Gravella, Miller, and Leary were sailing.

Ned, it had been regretfully decided, was too big. He and three other Dalesmen were to go along the bank on horseback trailing the pie-dish with ropes, while two others were to take the wagon back to Danby.

'I've a stool and a cushion or two in the wagon,' said Arthy, 'to make things a bit more comfortable.'

'And can I have a box to stand on?' asked Gravella. 'I shan't be able to see out if I don't.'

'Aye, I never thought of putting portholes,' said Jarge smartly, and the laugh rushed out again like a gale in the glade.

He good-naturedly went and fetched a sturdy wooden box and leaning over placed it in the pie-dish. Then, without warning, he put his hands under Gravella's arms and swung her up, high in the air, so that for a moment she seemed to be flying among the sun-splashed leaves and then whirring down like a bird. She blinked, put out a hand to steady herself, and was looking up at Jarge's delighted face over the rim of the pie-dish.

'My, you look small in there, little mistress,' he said. 'Can you catch an apple?'

He tossed one over the side and Gravella, running forward to catch it as it fell out of the sun and sky, forgot where she was, and set the dish rocking and see-sawing until her legs fell from under her and she lay sprawled on the flat, shining bottom. All around her rose the smooth, polished sides. This must be how a goldfish feels in a bowl, she thought. Then she got up and crawled over to her box where she sat carefully, picked up the apple and bit into it. The sharp juice ran on to her tongue. She looked up and saw only the blue sky and light green willow strands and was only saved from thinking she was dreaming by the sting of apple in her mouth.

As she stared up a leg appeared over the rim of the dish, then another, and Arthy dropped down in front of her as neatly as a nut. The dish rocked again. Farmer Leary's gaitered leg came over next, and then he too was asprawl and slithering as if he were on ice. Last of all came Miller, who fairly jumped in, and Gravella clung to her box with all her might and squealed out all the excitement that had been growing within her since cock-crow that morning.

Gingerly Arthy, Leary, and Miller got to their knees and then to their feet, careful to keep to the middle of the dish. Then they stood looking about them, delighted as schoolboys, taking in the never-before-felt sensation of being afloat in a pie-dish.

'Jarge,' called Arthy, 'are you there? Have you got the stool and cushions? And there's a red handkerchief with some bread and cheese.'

'Coming over,' called Jarge, and one by one the items were handed down and the sailors were stocked and comfortable for the voyage.

Leary and Miller could see over the edge, but Arthy stood on the stool and held on to the rim and Gravella mounted her box and saw the Dalesmen and Jarge lined up on the bank with proud, half-unbelieving faces. Two of them were untying the ropes from the willow and fastening them to their horses' bridles.

'Are you ready?' they called.

'Aye, aye!' shouted Arthy, waving vigorously. 'Cast her off, my lads.'

'Farewell!' shouted Jarge. 'A safe voyage to you!'

'Thanks, thanks!' called Arthy, and as he spoke the ropes tightened. The pie-dish turned slowly and gracefully and swung out into midstream.

We're afloat, thought Gravella. We really are afloat in a pie-dish. And I'm in history at this very minute. Me, Gravella Roller. I'm in history.

Chapter Thirteen

Gravella on her back in the pie-dish stared up at the sky and leaves. Gravella tip-toe on her box gazed down at the glinting water or watched the hilly moors unrolling, hot and still beneath a glaring sun. Soon the walls of the pie-dish grew almost too hot to touch and she had to fold a handkerchief and lay it on the rim so that she could hold on. The only sounds were the dry thudding of the horses' hooves on the hard-caked earth and the occasional hollow clang as the pie-dish struck a stone.

Leary had gone to sleep with the handkerchief over his face and Gravella felt sorry for him because he was sleeping while history was going on. Everywhere around was so quiet and deserted that it hardly seemed like history, but Gravella knew quite certainly that it was, and savoured every minute of it, remembering every detail so that she could tell it to her grandchildren.

Only once on the long, lazy voyage did they

see any human life. They had spread a shawl in
the bottom of the dish and unwrapped the bread
and cheese and a flask of milk, and were sitting
picnicking, so they did not see them at first . . .
Two small boys were sitting on a jutting grey
stone wall, fishing. Gravella saw their thin brown
legs when she heard their yells and looked up.
They called and threw stones until the dish had
passed, but the sailors were unconcerned and went
on munching.

'Their mothers'll never believe them when they
get home and say what they saw,' remarked
Arthy placidly. 'Jem'd never've believed you,
Gravella.'

And Gravella, pleasantly drowsy, agreed to
herself that that was certainly true.

The sky was all gold and red when the pie-dish
drew to the bank on the outskirts of the village.
The birds were beginning to whistle after the heat
of the day in a cool, echoing silence. Gravella
stretched herself and looked round for the last
time at the smooth, gleaming walls of the pie-
dish. I don't suppose I shall ever be inside a pie-
dish again, she thought.

The Dalesmen on horseback had dismounted
and were pulling on the ropes to bring the dish
right in under the cover of two great willows. So
Gravella felt first the fresh touch of their fronds

94

brushing her face, and then looked over the rim to see that they were enclosed within a wall of green hail, and even the sky had gone.

'Well,' said Arthy, his voice flat. 'Here we are, then.'

'Aye,' agreed Leary, getting stiffly to his feet.

Gravella felt chilly and shivered a little. She did not wish to be torn from the warmth of the dish, back to earth. She wanted to stay here for ever, and dreaded the sudden, sharp, breaking of the spell.

'We'll pass you up first, Gravella,' said Arthy. 'Are you there, you two?'

'Ready!' they replied, and again Gravella felt herself being lifted and swung up. There was a flash of green, a little bump, and she was standing knee-high in grass on the bank, her legs trembling a little, unused to the firmness of the ground beneath her. Arthy, Leary, and Miller all scrambled out in turn, and they all six of them stood silent, just watching the pie-dish as it lay rocking gently at its moorings. The reddish gleams of the setting sun lit the polished metal to splendour, and Gravella thought there could never have been a more noble vessel.

'Well,' said Arthy, 'best be getting along, I suppose. Who's staying guard?'

'We are,' volunteered the two Dalesmen. 'But

you might just ask our wives to run out to us
with a slice of pie and something to wet our
whistles. It'll be getting on for midnight before
you come for the dish.'

'Aye,' agreed Arthy, 'it will. We'll do that as
we go through the village.'

Gravella turned for one last look at the pie-
dish, and then they began to make their way
through the low-boughed trees and knee-high
grasses and then across a stretch of moor to the
road into Danby.

When Gravella got home she was given her
supper and then sent off upstairs to sleep for a few
hours before setting off to see the pie-dish on the
last stage of its journey to Leary's barn.

Jem woke her, and Gravella swung for a
moment between sleep and waking, wondering at
the darkness. She had not undressed, and at
Jem's bidding she crept quickly from under the
covers and put on her shoes.

'Put on your warmest shawl,' ordered Jem.
'And best put on a bonnet as well.'

Downstairs Arthy was waiting, fidgeting with
impatience to be off. He carried a large storm
lantern as high as his own knees.

'You won't be needing that,' said Jem, 'the
moon's come up as bright as day. This is more
likely what we'll be needing if there's trouble.'

She moved her hands under her cloak and the blade of the meat axe flashed alarmingly.

'Now there'll be no need for that, Jem,' said Arthy. 'There's twenty men going to fetch that dish, and no need for women to go waving meat axes about. Now put it down, or else don't come.'

Jem hesitated and then banged the axe on the table.

'I'll take your word, Arthy Roller,' she said. 'Now hurry, Gravella, we shall be late.'

They went out into the marvellously cold, fresh night, and walked over the rough cobbles that shone under the moon as if they were thick with hoar. On the green a group of dark cloaked figures were waiting by the largest hay-wain the Dale had to offer. They all climbed up and the horses set off with muffled hooves. They could not take the wagon right to the bank, and had to go the last fifty yards on foot.

Everything was silver and wet and there were strong green smells of river and dew-sodden earth and grass. Unseen creatures flurried through the undergrowth brushing grass and stirring stone. Owls hooted. Gravella held Jem's hand tightly and followed close behind Arthy.

At the bank they broke out into the full light of the moon. It lay over the Dan in broad silver bands and touched the pie-dish through the leaves of the overhanging trees, so that it seemed quite different, hollowed and shadowy, strangely mysterious. The Dalesmen who had not seen the dish before gasped and talked in hushed voices of the wonder of its size and beauty. For beautiful it was, lying there on that quiet water.

It seemed to Gravella that the tug-of-war that followed, with twenty Dalesmen heaving and straining to pull the pie-dish ashore, was undignified, and a poor ending to so noble a voyage. And it was hard work hacking a way through the boughs and bushes to drag the dish to where the wain stood. It was even harder work to lift the dish and balance it squarely and surely. Then it was lashed firmly with ropes to prevent it falling and squashing them like flies.

On the return journey the people walked behind the wagon watching the pie-dish go ahead like royalty. They were far too aware of the strangeness of it all to want to chatter. In silence the slow procession wound over the white moor road, and the great pie-dish came at last to Danby Dale by moonlight.

Chapter Fourteen

Jem was lamenting her lack of arithmetic for the thousandth time since the great pie had been thought of.

'We shall have to get Dame Toddy in,' she said. 'I'm that flummoxed I could weep. There's little black sticks and rings dancing round my poor head day and night, and Arthy never slept a wink last night. Muttering and counting, getting up to fetch the counters, crowding up slates with his doodling and drawing. Not a wink did the neither of us have.'

Gravella felt ashamed that her own arithmetic was not a little stronger so that she could help. But she never had cared much for sums, because they didn't seem to have much to do with living here on the free and blowing moors and making pies. So now she had been caught out, and she knew it served her right.

The Rollers' difficulty was that none of the recipes Arthy could lay his hands on mentioned a pie for anything near one thousand eaters, let alone two.

'It's the quantities,' he groaned. 'Miller's asking me how much flour I shall be needing, and Leary wants to know how many cattle. Not to mention herbs and onions and salt and—' he stopped.

'Pepper,' said Gravella without flinching. With the passing of time she had ceased to blame herself for the spoiling of the King's pie, and yet, oddly, in her heart she did not really blame Uncle Crispin either. Jem was the only one of the Rollers who really believed in his guilt, and Gravella sometimes wondered whether even she did not rant about him because she enjoyed it so much.

'We shall have to know by tomorrow,' said Arthy with decision. 'There's only seven days now to making, and the stuff's to be packed and carted.'

'Then Dame Toddy'll have to reckon it out,' said Jem. 'I ain't spending all the night again racking my brains to death, and that's a fact.'

So Gravella was sent with a recipe for two hundred and fifty eaters, to ask Dame Toddy to reckon the ingredients for two thousand.

Dame Toddy was watering the giant sunflowers along her garden wall. She was watering their roots because their great yellow faces waved and nodded so high that she had to stand on a chair to reach them with her watering pot.

Gravella explained the problem, and Dame Toddy nodded and led the way inside. They went into a tiny parlour, so decorated and so crammed with bits and pieces, with ships in bottles and embroidered mottoes and ladies made from shells, that Gravella could hardly keep her mind on what she was saying, so bemused was she by its crowded riches.

'Now, let's see,' said Dame Toddy, peering. 'That's times eight. Everything times eight.'

'That's what I told them,' cried Gravella eagerly, tearing her eyes away from a stuffed owl, fierce-eyed between two crinoline-lady thimble cases. 'I told them times eight!'

'I should think so, too,' said Dame Toddy severely. 'This is quite a simple problem, Gravella, and I'm surprised you couldn't work it out for yourself.'

She bent over a slate, muttering figures under her breath, and writing carefully. Gravella consoled herself by digging her toes deep into the fur rug and meeting boldly the gaze of a bead-eyed fox above the mantelshelf.

'Here,' said Dame Toddy at length. 'Take this to your father, Gravella, and tell him he may rely on it thoroughly. And tell him I wish him success in the great contest.'

'Thank you,' mumbled Gravella, and taking the slate she fled before Dame Toddy took it in her head to put her through her tables.

Back in the Roller kitchen she read out the list to Arthy and Jem.

'Two hundred pounds of flour.
One hundred pounds of lard.'

'Lawks!' cried Jem faintly.

'Two hundred pinches of salt.
Eight hundred teaspoonsful of water.'

'Would you *believe* it!' Jem's pinafore flew up above her head.

102

'That's the crust,' said Gravella. 'Now the filling.

> Two hundred pounds of steak.
> Seventy-five pounds of kidney.
> Fifty pounds of onions.
> Twelve and a half gallons of water.'

'Stop!' moaned Jem. 'I can't stand it. Do you hear, Arthy? What was it, twelve and a half gallons? Did you say, gallons, Gravella?'

'Gallons,' repeated Gravella. 'There'll have to be plenty of gravy, mother, for all those eaters.'

'But gallons!' fairly shrieked Jem. 'Arthy, you don't think we've gone and made a mistake, do you? You don't think we should have said five hundred eaters, and been satisfied? I can't believe this pie will *ever* get made. I can't, Arthy, though I try ever so hard.'

Arthy himself looked a little pale, but his hair burned the redder for it, and he sat very stiff and poised, as if ready to take off.

'This pie's going to be made, Jem,' he said, 'so don't you go worrying your head about that. I've made Standard Meats since I was twelve years old, and they're all the same, only some's little and some's bigger. This one's bigger, that's all.'

'What about herbs?' gabbled Jem, who hardly seemed to have heard his reassurances. 'Does it say about herbs, Gravella? Oooh, there's not time now to grow new ones, and my herbs don't stretch across the moors to Gorby, you know. There's only the one patch, outside the back door, and I've done my best with it, goodness only knows, but if there's going to be hundreds of pounds of this and hundreds of pounds of that going in, then there's going to be *handfuls* of herbs, handfuls and handfuls, and—'

'Jem!' Arthy held up his hand. 'Just you stop this minute. There's enough herbs of yours outside that back door for a pie for ten thousand eaters, let alone two, and I don't want to hear another word. And as for onions, I've two whole rows of them, and so has every other man in Danby, so there's no call to start on about them the minute you've finished with the herbs.'

Gravella saw, from the huge, gasping sigh of relief that Jem let out, that she had been about to 'start on' about onions the minute she had regained her breath.

For the rest of that day Jem wandered about her kitchen in an aimless, staring-eyed sort of way, and Gravella would hear her mutter under her breath, 'Gallons. All them *gallons*.' Or, 'Eight hundred teaspoonsful. *Hundred!* Teaspoonsful!'

Her voice rising each time, until it seemed to come right out of the top of her head.

After dinner Arthy went down to the village to tell Leary and Miller that the quantities were reckoned.

'They didn't seem that surprised,' he told Jem at supper. 'Leary reckons he thought he'd have had to use his whole herd. He reckons he'll have a few left.'

'That shows how much they know about pie-making,' sniffed Jem, but Gravella knew that she was trying, in her prickly way, to cover up her gratitude for the kindness of men like Farmer Leary who would sacrifice a herd of cattle to the dream of a pie.

But the pie, which until now, despite all the preparations, had seemed only a dream, was suddenly real and near, so that Gravella could almost see it rising above that giant dish and smell its gravy in swirling gallons and imagine herself standing in its shadows.

Five days to the making, not counting today, six to the contest. Only four to the measuring and herb-crushing. Gravella's mouth went suddenly dry. It was almost too much to bear.

Chapter Fifteen

On the day before the great contest Gravella opened her eyes, lay for a minute or two staring up at the black beams, and then suddenly found herself forced to close them again. She opened them a second time and blinked rapidly, feeling her eyes smart. Below in the kitchen she could hear a dull, regular chopping.

'The onions!' cried Gravella, and next minute she was out of bed and throwing open the window and leaning out as far as she could, snuffing in the cold heathery scent of the moorland breeze.

'The pie's begun to be made,' chanted Gravella to a soaring lark. 'The pie's begun to be made!'

She dressed quickly and ran downstairs. The minute she opened the kitchen door the full strength of the chopped onions met her and she groped straight across and out at the back door, where she opened her eyes and gulped in mouthfuls of air. Jem was unconcernedly chopping, nimbly turning her knife and humming jerkily under her breath. Her own eyes were wide and tearless. She was wearing her grandmother's locket.

'Ten pounds chopped already, Gravella,' she sang out. 'Only forty more!'

'Forty!' cried Gravella in consternation. 'But where shall I live all day? I can't live in this house full of onion smoke! It's burning my eyes already!'

'You can go down to the barn and help Arthy,' replied Jem, still chopping. 'I shall be chopping all morning, perhaps longer. And I don't want my enjoyment spoilt by your complainings, Gravella. I enjoy a good chop, and I don't suppose I shall ever have such a good one again, so I mean to make the most of it. Now just take a bit of what you fancy out of the larder and get straight down to the barn, there's a good girl.'

Thankfully Gravella did as she was told. When she reached the meadow she could tell that something was amiss. Groups of people stood talking excitedly and waving their hands, and as she hurried past them once or twice she thought she heard the word 'Gorby'.

She entered the barn without even having to give the password. So high and wide was it that even the dozen or so people inside seemed tiny and hardly noticeable. Enormous trestle tables ran

107

down the sides and in the centre stood the great dish itself, very still and dim, as if sleeping, waiting to come to life.

The next minute the pie-dish was forgotten as she saw the cause of all the excitement. Cousin Bates was here! His eyes were red with blubbing and he was every now and then rubbing his eyes and sniffing.

'What has happened?' she cried. 'Why is Bates here, father?'

'Best ask him,' said Arthy. 'Caught snooping just before sun-up.'

'I wasn't snooping,' cried Bates. 'I was mushrooming.'

'In June?' asked Arthy. 'Now, Bates, you know better than that.'

'The question is, what's to be done with him,' said Ned thoughtfully. 'He can't be let go, that's certain.'

'I want to go home,' said Bates sullenly. 'Father'll be looking for me. He'll come for me, you see.'

'Oh, so he knew where you were, did he?' said Leary sharply. 'Perhaps he was here with you?'

'Now, Bates, there's no need to take on,' said Arthy, seeing his nephew's face beginning to rumple again. 'No one's going to do you any harm. You'll be well fed and looked after. We just can't have you going back to Gorby and blabbing what you've seen, that's all.'

'I haven't seen anything,' cried Bates eagerly, his eyes lighting for a moment with the hope of reprieve. 'I haven't seen anything, and I won't tell a soul, honest.'

Arthy hesitated.

'No,' said Ned firmly. 'I say no.'

And the knot of Dalesmen murmured their agreement.

'Tomorrow morning when we wheel this pie out, then you go too. Not before.'

'It won't be so bad, Bates,' said Gravella, herself a little sorry for her woebegone cousin. 'You'll be able to watch the pie made, and that'll be history. I shall be here watching it too.'

'Pie?' said Bates disbelievingly. 'You're really going to make the pie in here? In a barn?'

'In that very dish,' said Arthy, not without pride, nodding in its direction.

'Dish? I don't see no dish,' said Bates.

Leary rapped his knuckles on the polished sides.

'Here,' he said.

Bates's eyes stretched with astonishment. His face began to redden and his cheeks puffed out until Gravella thought he must certainly burst. Then, suddenly, he sat down and deflated like a balloon. For a moment he sat there staring. Then,

'You're going to make a pie in that?' he shrieked. 'In *that*?'

'That's about the size of it,' agreed Arthy. 'What do you think of that, then?'

But Bates again was speechless. It must be like a dream come true for him, Gravella thought. He must have dreamed of a pie like that.

Just then the barn door burst open and Miller rushed in, a windmill of arms and legs.

'Arthy,' he gasped, 'there's trouble. There's your brother Crispin from Gorby outside and his missis, and they're wanting to see you. And they're raging terrible.'

'I'll come,' said Arthy. 'You wait here, Bates.'

Bates did not even hear. He was gazing at the pie-dish, mouth ajar, deaf to the world.

Gravella and Arthy stepped out into the sunlit meadow. They saw Crispin and Essie standing by, faces frowning, and they saw, too, a familiar figure striding through the clover, a basket in each hand. It was Jem with another batch of her refreshments. Arthy closed his eyes in anguish, then opened them and went manfully towards the outraged Gorby Rollers.

'Now then, Arthy,' began Crispin immediately. 'We won't stand wasting words. I'll have my boy back and we'll be off to Gorby. There's a pie to be made and I've no time to stand arguing.'

'Though we might ask what you mean by taking our poor boy a prisoner and holding the innocent child against his will,' put in Essie, 'we *might*.'

'We might,' said Crispin, 'but we won't. We'll just take the boy and be off. I've no wish to quarrel with you, Arthy, and we won't dwell on the matter.'

'Dwell?' It was Jem's voice, high and angry as a wasp's. 'Don't you stand there talking about dwelling, Crispin Roller. *We're* the ones who're entitled to go dwelling on things, if there's any dwelling to be done. And what's this I hear about that Bates come snooping and spying in the black of night when folks is in their beds? Answer me that!'

'That boy was out walking,' said Crispin with dignity. 'We all was, as a matter of fact. It was a fine moonlight night and we went walking. That's no crime.'

'Walking!' Jem said. 'Eight miles from Gorby! That Bates can't walk from one side of the room to the other without puffing and blowing fit to blow an old man's candles out. Don't you go telling me about him walking!'

'Now I know you're holding against us what happened to—' began Crispin.

'Sssssh!' hissed Arthy. The Dalesmen standing around had their ears cocked and the honour of the Rollers lay in the secret that Crispin had nearly given away.

'You know what,' said Crispin, seeing his mistake. 'And I tell you on my solemn word, Jem, that that was a mistake, pure and simple, and no doing of mine. A Roller doesn't stoop to them kind of tricks.'

'A Danby Roller don't,' said Jem.

'Nor any Roller, Jem.' It was Arthy, speaking with decision. 'That whole matter's dead and buried, Crispin, and here's my hand on it.'

The two men solemnly shook hands while the two ladies quivered and itched.

'So now, Arthy, we'll just take Bates and be getting along,' said Crispin. 'There's pie-making to be done by the both of us—and may the best man win.'

'He will,' said Jem dangerously.

'He'll have to promise on his word not to tell what he's seen,' said Arthy, 'then he can go.' He raised his voice. 'Bates! Bates! Come out here, now. Your father and mother are come to fetch you back to Gorby.'

They waited. Nothing happened.

'Bates!' bellowed Crispin. 'Come out here this minute!' The door of the barn opened and Leary came out.

'He won't come,' he said.

112

'What!' screamed Essie. 'Won't what?'

'Won't come,' said Leary. 'He says he's stopping, and no one shall make him budge till tomorrow.'

'Well!' said Crispin, crestfallen, feeling rather silly at coming to release a prisoner who preferred to stay in prison.

'I ain't so sure we want him,' said Jem, looking pleased at Crispin's discomfiture nevertheless. 'Do we, Arthy? Snooping and spying.'

'He can stop for me,' said Arthy. 'Crispin's his father.'

'I'm stopping here!' It was Bates's voice, loud and defiant from the jaws of the barn. 'I'm not coming!'

Crispin looked worried. Gravella could see that he was wondering what undreamed of secret the barn held that could make his son act so strangely. Essie burst into tears.

'It's witchcraft!' she sobbed. 'That's what it is! My mother always said her—' she stabbed a finger full of rings at Jem—'grandmother was a witch!'

'Perhaps she was,' nodded Jem placidly, enjoying herself.

Crispin seemed to make up his mind suddenly.

'Come along, Essie,' he said in a very loud voice. 'If the lad wants to stop he shall. And tomorrow he can *walk* back to Gorby himself. For we shan't have time to come running after him.'

113

He waited, head cocked, to see the effect of his words.

Nothing happened. The crease on Uncle Crispin's forehead deepened to a rut.

'Come along, Essie!' he snapped. 'I'll be seeing you tomorrow, Arthy, at the contest.'

Essie turned as they went and shrieked over her shoulder, 'And no witchcraft! Fair play!'

Jem's laughter, rarely heard but magnificent, filled the ten acre and scattered skylarks heavenward.

And then they all went in to start the pie-making.

Chapter Sixteen

Arthy used rain-water butts for pastry bowls. He measured the flour and fat into each one and spent most of the morning rubbing them. Jem had suggested that he might allow someone to help him with the task, but he had rejected the idea firmly.

'Never,' he said, rubbing a floury hand through his hair until the red was streaked with white. 'A crust must have the touch of a butterfly, and it's something you're born with, like green eyes or a wart on your nose. This pastry's having the Roller touch, and no other.'

So he worked over the butts, up to the elbows in pastry, eager as a mole. Jem went back up to the house to finish her chopping and brood over her herbs.

Leary had been entrusted with the cooking of the meat. At any rate, he was allowed to watch to make sure it didn't boil over or catch the bottom of the cauldrons. He paced up and down like a sentry on guard, lifting lids, peering, stirring, sniffing. Twenty cauldrons there were in all, simmering in a row, spurting steam that grew more fragrant as the day wore on and set poor Bates into a flood of mouthwatering. Gravella was constantly handing him cakes and patties to stem the flow and he ate them absently, his fingers stuffing his mouth mechanically while his eyes followed Arthy with something like worship.

'It's ready for rolling,' said Arthy at last, straightening his back. 'On to the table with it.'

The table was one that had been made specially for the rolling. Its measurements were just the same as those of the top of the pie-dish, so that it could be fitted exactly and Arthy could roughly trim the edges before actually putting it on the pie.

Half a dozen Dalesmen stepped forward and rolled the butts to the centre of the barn. Then each was heaved up above the table and the pastry turned out in huge, soft mountains.

Arthy climbed up on to the table and knelt there, pressing the pastry down. Then Leary handed him the rolling pin, made specially two feet long and thick as a man's arm, and the rolling began. Two hours it took before the pastry lay smooth and even, fitting the table top perfectly like a fall of snow.

He had not even noticed Jem come in with her baskets of herbs. He did not see Gravella counting teaspoonsful of salt and pepper and then recounting and counting them again. When Arthy made a crust the world could stop turning and stand on its head and he would not turn a single orange hair.

Now he stepped back and stared fiercely at his handiwork, squinting this way and that to find out any unevenness or flaw.

'It'll do,' he said briefly at last. 'Now for the real work. Where are the trimmings?'

Miller stepped forward carrying a huge earthenware bowl.

'There, Arthy,' he said, 'I've been keeping them cool for you over yon.'

'Oh, no, you don't,' said Jem sweeping forward. 'Not one touch of that pastry do you have until you've eaten and drank and got your strength, Arthy Roller. Once you get started on them trimmings *nothing* will stop you, that I do know.'

So Arthy was made to sit down and put away bread and cheese and a slab of fruit pie. He did not speak at all and his eyes did not move from the bowl of pastry.

Jem collected up her things and once more set off back to the house. Arthy, like a released prisoner, sprang back to his feet and within a minute was back in his world of pastry. For three hours he worked on the centrepiece while the Dalesmen tiptoed round the barn and talked in hushed voices, aware of the intensity of Arthy's vision. The light was beginning to fade and someone lit three lanterns and placed them nearby, though Arthy himself did not even notice. With the falling of night the pie-dish loomed and grew and took on a life of its own, an air of brooding expectancy.

At last Arthy put down his knife and stepped back. The stillness in the barn gathered and thickened.

Then, 'It's done,' Arthy said. And he turned his back and walked away.

The Dalesmen came and gathered round it, awed and exclaiming. It had been decided that as this was not strictly a Roller pie but a pie of the Dale, the old Roller traditions did not apply, and the crust could be seen by any who cared to look. In any case, Gravella thought, Arthy would never have lifted the crust on to the pie single-handed, so either the traditions went or the pie did.

Now the time had come for the filling to be ladled into the pie-dish itself. A pair of step-ladders was placed by its side and a chain of men passed bowls of the stew, still faintly steaming, from hand to hand. The last man, perched on the top step, emptied the contents into the pie-dish with a soft, thick splash. For an hour they worked while the darkness deepened and more and more lanterns sprang into life until the barn was filled with moving light and huge, swaying shadows like giants on the white-washed walls. There was very little noise. The excitement was deep-running like an undercurrent in a quiet river.

The last bowl was handed up. The man on the step-ladders dismounted and the chain broke. Little excited huddles formed and all eyes were on the pastry table.

Arthy and two helpers then began the first delicate steps towards moving the crust to the pie. They took a thinly beaten sheet of metal and began to slide it very gently between the pastry and the table. Gravella saw that it was almost the exact width of the table, but had handles at each side, to make moving easier. There were three metal sheets in all, so that the crust could be lowered on to the pie gradually in three stages, and not 'dropped all at once, hit or miss', as Arthy said.

Arthy held up his hand and the group of men who were to help him with the actual covering of the pie stepped forward, wide-eyed in the jumping light. Gravella knew that this was the most important moment of all. All the men holding the metal trays had to keep their parts absolutely level with the rest. If one man let his part drop, or lifted it too high, then the pastry would break and the crust be torn. Those great, clumsy Dalesmen, with their thick fingers and booted feet, lifted that crust as if it were glass beaten to snapping thinness. They went towards the pie-dish tip-toe and jaws ajar, staring-eyed, breath held, slowly, half adread. As the first three men lifted the trays to their shoulders ready to slide them over the top of the dish, Gravella shut her eyes, content to be a coward. There was a slow, soft scraping, a long sigh from the watchers, and Gravella opened her eyes to see the pie capped, looking at last like a real pie, nearly a thousand times larger than life. Arthy, edging round it perched on ladders, fussing over the edges, looked like Tom Thumb in the giant's pantry. Bates let out a long-held breath in a huge gasping breeze.

Satisfied at last Arthy came down and with Miller's help began the last stage of that prodigious making. Gently the two men slid the sheet of metal under that exquisite centrepiece, so that not a curl, not a flourish was disturbed. And as carefully they carried it to the dish and set it at last in the middle of that wide white crust, the crowning perfection. As Arthy climbed down a soft perceptible sigh ran through the shadowy barn and all the toil of the day gathered into this one moment of achievement. The pie was ready for the oven.

Suddenly Arthy changed. His frozen, white face, set into the concentration of the artist, relaxed. He was all workman now, busy and practical, giving orders. He tested the temperature of the oven and called for volunteers for wheeling in the pie. As the wide doors of the oven swung open a warm blast of air blew against Gravella's cheeks and the candle flames bowed as if in salute. Swiftly the pie-dish was rolled forward and into the darkness of the oven. The doors clanged to and the pie had gone.

The barn looked strangely vacant and for the first time that night Gravella thought how odd it was to be in a barn at nearly midnight, with half the Dale around her instead of asleep in their beds under the quiet moon. Tomorrow night the barn would be a barn again, blank and still in the moonlit acres of the meadow, with only the bats and mice to cross its silent shadows. Her head drooped lower.

'Gravella!' It was Jem shaking her shoulder. 'Come along now, child, back to your bed.'

Gravella protested sleepily, 'But the tasting. I want to see the pie come out.'

'You won't be seeing anything whether you stay or go,' said Jem. 'Half-asleep and white as chalk. Get up, now.'

Gravella stumbled to her feet to find that her legs would scarcely hold her. She rubbed her eyes and swayed and as she did so she felt herself being lifted by a pair of strong arms and felt rough cloth against her cheek.

'I'll carry her up to the house for you,' she heard Ned's voice say from a long way off. 'The child's half-asleep.'

She felt the cool air on her face as they left the

barn, and once opened her eyes to see the moon hanging over Ned's ear and stars over his shoulder. She sometimes knew that feet were thudding on moor turf and a gate was being opened and then boards creaked. Last of all she was enveloped by enormous warmth and softness into which she swam neither knowing nor caring if it was her own bed or the wide arms of sleep itself.

Chapter Seventeen

At breakfast next morning the Rollers could hear the sound of horses' hooves and wheels over the stones and could scarcely eat for choking excitement. Even Bates, who had slept on a bale of straw in the barn so that he should not miss the pie coming out of the oven, ate less than usual. The pie, Arthy assured Jem and Gravella, was perfect.

'It was Standard Meat,' said he wonderingly, 'and I've made it a thousand times before, but I tell you, Jem, it tasted better than any I've ever made. It was the same recipe—times eight, of course—but I tell you it tasted different.'

'Bound to,' said Jem. 'You can't bake a pie for a king and it not taste different. That's what I told you before, but you wouldn't listen. But I'm not the one to say, "I told you so".'

'You were right, Jem,' said Arthy generously. He could afford to be generous. The whole glorious sunlit day was stretching before him like a golden sea on which to launch his pie. His hair was fairly crackling with fire.

The judging was to take place at eleven o'clock in the very meadow in which the barn stood, chosen because of its size and because the King was staying with the Baron in the Hall nearby.

Gravella dressed in her spotted muslin and best straw bonnet and then went dutifully to Jem for inspection. Jem herself was wearing red. A dull, damped down, smouldering red, to be sure, but red nevertheless, and a very daring step for her. Gravella thought it suited her better than the greys and browns and blacks she always chose, and told her so.

'I don't know,' said Jem, pressing the skirts down with her big red hands, 'I still think it looks a bit on the *forward* side. More the kind of thing that Essie goes in for.'

Arthy wore the suit he kept for church and Christmas, but his white face and orange hair were so crackling and alight and his whole person so quivering and dancing and unable to be contained, that what he wore was of no importance whatever. So the three Rollers and Dog set off across the moors, which was the shortest cut.

The meadow had mushroomed overnight with gay stalls and panoplies. There was a dais for the

King, splashed scarlet like an early poppy. Stalls were selling trinkets and favours, ribbons, laces, drinks of ale, and candies. Dalesmen and their families sat munching on the grass, resting after a drive through the night of thirty miles and more. The pies themselves were lined up on trestle tables, sixteen of them. And ours makes seventeen, thought Gravella, bigger than all the others put together.

'Just look there,' hissed Jem, stabbing Arthy in the ribs. 'Just look at that Essie how she's freaked herself up! Oh my, let's hope the King don't see her!'

Aunt Essie had put on all her jewellery in honour of the occasion and the effect was tremendous. She was hardly to be seen for rings and bangles and necklets and brooches. She flashed and shimmered as the sun struck her, and Gravella thought the effect pretty from a distance, and Jem's own single opal brooch rather severe by contrast. Loyally she checked the thought.

It was easy to see why Aunt Essie was so delighted with herself, for at very first glance the Gorby Dale pie stood out as at any rate the biggest, if not the best.

'That's the two hundred recipe,' said Arthy after an expert glance. 'There's none other over a hundred and fifty. Oh, pinch me, Jem, I must be dreaming. Ten times bigger than any here, that's what ours is. Ten times! I could have made one for only a thousand and still carried the show.'

'Two thousand's just right,' said Jem decisively. 'One thousand's good, but two's better. Just right.'

Suddenly the crowd swayed and moved as if in a wind, and Gravella saw that the King was coming. He rode on a horse of pure white and banners of scarlet embroidered with gold fluttered round him. His hair was as red as Arthy's own.

It's a sign, thought Gravella, and as quickly checked the thought. She did not want any signs, because they smacked of witchery, and even here in broad daylight in the meadow thick with trampled clover, witchery was not a thing to be tinkered with.

The notes of the bugles went shining through the air and left behind them a silence that only the skylarks did not mark. And, as always when there has been a great silence, no one dared to be the first to speak, and so the King and his party began to pass along the row of pies in silence. One by one they were tasted, a slice of each being placed on a golden plate and handed to the King, who tried a morsel, neck arched, red comb of hair flaming, like a cockerel, Gravella thought. Very very slowly, like a wave gathering, first whispering, then murmuring, and then excited talking broke out among the crowd. Everyone strained to catch a glimpse of the King's face as he tasted, trying to read his judgement there. But he tasted the sixteenth pie and no one in the whole meadow dared guess the answer, and as he stood hesitating a great cry went up:

'The Danby Dale pie! Where's the Danby Dale pie!'

Delicately the King's eyebrows arched and the doors of the barn opened slowly on great groaning hinges. There was sudden silence. Out from the shadows came the huge pie-dish, wheeled by twenty men with straining shoulders. The sun fell for the first time on to that glorious crust, perfectly smooth and brown, gleaming faintly. It was impossible, a miracle under that blue sky, standing among the grass and clover like some enormous fruit. It was seen and yet impossible to believe.

No one could speak for the wonder of it. Gravella could feel her own tongue cleaving to the roof of her mouth and her eyes stinging. Arthy was rigid, locked in awe. Though he had created it last night in the shadows of the barn, yet he could hardly believe it in the glare of sunlight. For a full minute the pie stood there and more than three thousand people stood and stared in silence, made

into statues by their disbelief. Then the roar that broke out sent the skylarks somersaulting skyward and the din broke in deafening fragments and Arthy was borne up into the air and shouldered to the King. Gravella could see him, hair in tongues of flame, level with his own pie-crust, white and dazed with pride, and Jem kept saying, 'Look, oh look! Look! Just look!'

Arthy said afterwards that he didn't really remember the King giving him the purse at all. Jem would sit cross-examining him for hours, but he never budged.

'I tell you I don't remember, Jem,' he would say.

'But you must remember something, Arthy,' Jem would wail. 'Think, now, didn't he say something when he gave you the purse?'

'I believe he did, Jem,' Arthy would say. 'But I don't even remember him giving me the purse, so I can't rightly say.'

'*Oh, Arthy!*' and she would start off all over again, determined to salvage some tiny shred to be handed down through the Rollers and repeated to Essie when the Gorby Rollers next came by.

Jem's gown of sombre red caught fire as the day went on and she flashed through the meadow like a bird, awhirl with happiness and pride. Every single person there had a slice of the Danby pie, and many saved their portion in a handkerchief to take home and preserve, like a pressed petal. They were ordinary people and had never in their whole lives seen history made, so they wanted a memento to assure them that they had not imagined it all. Five or ten or fifteen winters in the Dales would make today only a far-off dream without the jar of pickled pie to give it substance.

Bates had seven portions and spent the day in bliss. He never moved from the shadow of the dish but sprawled in the dry grass licking his gravied fingers or snoring gently.

Crispin and Essie came to give their congratulations, swallowing their own disappointment as best they could. That day Gravella came near to liking them.

'I near fainted, Arthy, that's a fact,' said Crispin. He was, after all, a Roller and a piemaker, and loved pies nearly as well as Arthy himself. 'Never did I expect to see the like. I tell you I near dropped. This is a proud day for the Rollers, Arthy, a proud day.'

'It is certainly a large pie,' said Essie, who was determined not to appear put out by Arthy's victory, but equally determined not to seem unduly impressed. 'I must say it seemed to me rather ordinary as far as *taste* goes, but I suppose one can't have quality *and* quantity. No doubt his Majesty realized that.'

Jem let this remark go entirely unchallenged and Gravella was proud of her.

They did not leave the meadow till dusk and as they walked back over the moor the grass was beginning to smell of dew and one or two stars were out. No one spoke, each was tight in his own thoughts. When they entered the kitchen and lighted the lamps, it seemed as if they had been away for a thousand years. Jem unwrapped the slab of pie she had brought up for supper and put it on the table. All three of them stood looking at it.

'I think perhaps it could have done with just a shade more parsley,' said Jem meditatively.

'Oh, I wouldn't say that, Jem,' said Arthy. 'I thought it was just about exact as regards parsley. As regards all seasonings for that matter, Jem. It was beautiful seasoning, Jem.'

Jem blushed. Tall, bony, and corseted as she was, she could blush like a nymph.

'The crust, though,' went on Arthy meditatively. 'I ain't so sure but what I've done better. As regards texture, I mean. The trimmings was all right, I suppose.'

'All right!' Jem's voice began to rise. 'When I saw them trimmings, a shiver went up me right from my toes. They was *beautiful*, Arthy. I shall never forget them trimmings as long as I live.

Not if I live to be a hundred and ten, like my grandmother did.'

'But the texture, Jem,' Arthy persisted. 'Here, hand me a piece now. I might have been mistaken. But next time . . .'

Gravella smiled and tiptoed away. There would, of course, be a next time. Arthy Roller was back in pie-making again. And Jem and Arthy would sit there half the night going over and over the making of the pie from beginning to end. Recipe books would be dragged out from the shelves and consulted, past pies resurrected, and Arthy might even have to go back down to the meadow after midnight to fetch another piece of pie for tasting.

As she lay on her back staring at the black beams and the moonlight fettered in the cobwebs, Gravella could hear their excited voices coming up from the kitchen. Even in her sleep she heard them.

In the ten acre the giant pie, guarded by two snoring Dalesmen, lay on a lake of silver. Moonlight poured through its shattered crust and the moon itself was reflected in the gravy. If Gravella had seen it, tired though she was, she would have realized that this, too, was history. But she was asleep, and past caring, and history had to go on without her.

Epilogue

Plenty of things happened to the Danby Rollers after the making of the Great Pie, but this seemed a good place to stop, because smaller pies, however interesting in their own way, would be bound to fall rather flat by comparison.

It might occur to some of you to doubt the truth of some of this story—the *historical truth*, I mean. Those readers I advise to go up to Danby Dale one day and to look very closely at the duck pond on the village green. To begin with, it is oblong instead of round, in itself a suspicious circumstance. It was this, along with Jarge the blacksmith's own jokes about the pie-dish, that first made me go down on my hands and knees in the rather muddy grass around the edge, and examine it very carefully.

I was quite right. It *is* the pie-dish, and to my mind it is a far more poetic end for it to be there, full of water and weeds and ducks, than hung up in some gloomy museum among breastplates and Roman coins and stuffed birds. I think Arthy must have thought of it.

Other Oxford fiction

The Bongleweed
Helen Cresswell
ISBN 0 19 275032 1

Warning—Bongleweed on the loose!

The Bongleweed plant is weird and wonderful, and it grows faster than *anything*! Becky tricks stuck-up Jason into sprinkling some seeds in Pew Gardens—but fun soon turns to fear as a bushy Bongleweed jungle springs up, with no sign of stopping.

Before long, the Gardens and local graveyard are completely covered—and now the Bongleweed is heading for the rest of the village! It's up to Becky and Jason to stop the wickedly wild weed before it's too late . . .

A magically funny story from the award-winning author of *The Bagthorpe Saga*.

How to Survive Summer Camp
Jacqueline Wilson
ISBN 0 19 275019 4

Typical! Mum and Uncle Bill have gone off on a swanky honeymoon, while Stella's been dumped at Evergreen Summer Camp. Guess what? She's not happy about it!

Things get worse. Stella loses all her hair (by accident!), has to share a dorm with snobby Karen and Louise, and is forced into terrifying swimming lessons with Uncle Pong! It looks as if she's in for a nightmare summer—how can Stella possibly survive?